THE PETERLOO INHERITANCE

Josiah and Sarah Ayesthorpe have been married for over twenty years. Their son Adam has been ordered from the family home by his father, their daughter Maureen is involved in a secret relationship with a man her parents could never approve of.

It is the time come to be known as the hungry forties; the town is crippled by strikes, hunger and destitution are rife, but so is courage.

Courage in the form of Jane Marsden who wants more from life than her situation promises and courage too in the form of Richard Jones a *foreigner* to Manchester come to make his way and knowing that the only way he is going to succeed is by hard manual work.

The Peterloo Inheritance

by

M. Glaiser Blake

ROBERT HALE · LONDON

ISBN 0 7091 9000 X

Robert Hale Ltd
Clerkenwell House
Clerkenwell Green
London EC1R 0HT

Photoset by Rowland Phototypesetting Ltd
Printed in Great Britain by St Edmundsbury Press
Bury St Edmunds, Suffolk
Bound by Redwood Burn Ltd

In Memory of Jack Pinnington
A fine man and a good friend

One

The river had the colour of uncooked liver, thick and dark and giving off an unpalatable odour. It lay almost still, barely flowing as if it were a stagnant pool. Rumour had it that should you fall into any of the rivers of the town, the Irwell, the Irk or the Medlock you would perish from instantaneous poisoning before drowning, even should you be able to swim, the thick polluted water would bring about your end before you reached the nearest bank.

The building, he saw, backed onto the bank of the river, before it in this warren of crumbling masonry, the road was unpaved and because of the recent rain the earth ran in loose rivers of deep dark mud, together with animal and human excretia. The piles of manure were left until there were sufficient amounts to make it a saleable commodity by the landlords who owned these rat holes, called homes to the majority of the town's labour.

For a moment overcome by an equal proportion of disgust and anger he leant against the wall of number four, the dwelling he sought, then when the fastidious side of his nature—never a small unimportant part—got the better of him he moved away, angrily brushing the shoulders of his impeccable lovat greatcoat.

A pig passed by, its snout ferreting amongst the piles of obscene debris with happy innocence, looking at it, his mind screamed the question, "Who are these people, what are the names of those who own these properties, who allow themselves to degrade others?" and then he

7

trembled because he knew. Knew that once his own family had been part of it, and shuddered in the horror of knowing that some of his own family were still at the centre of it, though thank God he was not. He had rid himself of it all but, his conscience, never a still thing, taunted him with the rememberance that he had rid himself of it at a substantial profit.

The building was of three storeys with cellars. People—families—lived in the cellars; the floors were of earth and when it rained these were turned into mud. In the cellar of this building the Marsdens lived. Joe, his wife, two children and his sister Jane, who had by good fortune and the offices of a gentleman from the Cross Street chapel, obtained a job in service.

He climbed to the top of the building, along dirty stairs where wood was splintering because of a concentrated attack of woodworm, age and the elements. The stench of overcooked cabbage crawled from every door, or so it seemed, and the wail or the cough of a sick child rendered a symphony of such wretchedness it made him pause and retch. That people had to live in these conditions was a deplorable reality, but that someone should choose to do so when there was no need seemed no more than masochism.

The door like the others was of warped wood. He knocked, from within came murmurs and a sharp retort that was indiscernible and then the door opened.

The man opened the door himself. Tall, thin and fair with eyes like crushed violets, eyes that never failed to arouse feelings in the breasts of all that saw them. Sometimes sad, sometimes gay, now as angry as an impending storm cloud.

"Father," he said, and had he said Satan or killer or any of the many adjectives in his vocabulary, none could have sounded more vicious. This was his son, flesh of his

8

flesh, indisputedly his. The cheekbones, the hair, the mouth and nose, all grafted miraculously from his seed, his own child grown in the belly of the woman he loved, but now a man, a man alone and one indeed who inexplicably hated him. His eyes—*her eyes*—met and matched his, a game that lasted only seconds but might have been of longer duration for all the tensions it awakened.

"I would like to talk to you," his father said, "I think it important."

"To who?"

"To your mother."

Ah, a flicker of emotion, a softening here and there, the downward slope of eyebrows.

"All right," Adam said, opening the door wider so that his father could step into the room.

This then was his son's home, this one room whose solitary window looked down onto the liver-coloured Irwell. Here he slept, ate and cooked. Small and cramped and dominated by an easel and canvas. Apart from the tools of his profession there was a tiny table, and two chairs, an ornate screen and a bed.

A girl was lounging on the bed. She had lots of brown hair that tumbled around her, and pale blue eyes. A pretty enough girl in a voluptuous kind of way. She was wearing only a blue robe, carelessly tied, and appeared not at all embarrassed that she showed, to a stranger, areas of her body like thigh, calf and breast.

"My father," Adam said, "this is Rosie."

No explanation, his father had not expected any, father and son had been at war for so long now that it was something both had grown used to. Their war had culminated on a September evening, neither would be able to forget it, and this was their first meeting since that night.

"You'd better go," his son said to the girl, "you can come back later if you like."

Rosie unwound herself, bestowed a smile upon Josiah of an obvious kind and then left without a word. He was a little surprised because he had expected her to be living with his son, and was oddly relieved to discover she was not.

His son had been painting Rosie without her robe. He glanced at the picture surreptitiously because he knew how much Adam loathed him to see any of his work. Although he painted and painted exceedingly well there was a difference about their work. In Adam's there was a hint of madness, of self-torture. Josiah painted with his mind but his son, he now came to realize, painted from the very depths of his soul.

Adam it would seem, had to paint, he would not compromise, would not paint in the evening while working by day, could not snatch an hour here, or there, with him it had to be always. Everything else had to come second. Yet it had not been this that had caused that night.

Because of his once romantic ideas he had fought for his son's right to paint, and had been unbeknown to Adam his champion, just as much as his mother had.

What then had caused the vitriol to spill, what had happened that his son saw things so wrong? What had warped him, and turned him into a person of such bitterness that his father had thought never to speak with him again.

It had been a misunderstanding. Grandfather had been interfering as usual, demanding to have his own way and becoming obdurate when he realized his son would not give in.

He wanted Adam at the hub of his industrial empire. It did not matter that he had his son, and his own daugh-

10

ter's son in the business, he wanted Adam.

There was a lot of bitterness in the family because of his attitude. He loved Adam above all the others, making no secret of the fact that Josiah's son was his favourite, hardly paying any attention to young George Littlemoss and his brother Frank. It was *all* Adam, even though young George had all the characteristics for business. He wanted Adam, blind and uncaring of the fact that had become obvious to everyone else, that Adam was—depending upon who in the family was viewing him—lazy or artistic.

That day the old man had given his son hell. Josiah had not, because of his father's age, said very much, only now in the confines of his home did he feel able to give vent to his feelings, especially since the grandparents were going to pay a visit that very evening.

"As if I do not have enough of him all day he must come in the evening," he had complained to his wife. He was not shouting at her, he was *not*! He was merely releasing tension by speaking over loudly. She knew that, sitting quietly because had he been shouting at her she was quite capable of shouting back. Even Maureen, his daughter, was aware of the true facts, then why oh why did his son misconstrue the situation, or was it that he had been looking only for an excuse to vocally attack him.

"Your son, madam, your son, not anyone else's, the finest fellow in the whole land might apply for a position but he only wants what he cannot have. Why I ask myself, why your son? I can only come to one conclusion," she looked up at him, "do not deny it," he said.

"How dare you speak to my mother like that!"

They turned, watching as he strode into the room. Mother half stood, changed her mind and sat once more.

Josiah thought of the hours he had had to suffer listen-

11

ing to his father's ravings, how he had protected his son's right to live a life away from the factory and warehouse, away from the deafening clamour of the loom and the stink of the town with its sewage problems and smoking chimneys, and for his trouble he received in return cold contempt, indifference and none of the respect he had been brought up to believe you gave to a parent as a right.

"I beg your pardon?" Josiah said.

"I said how dare you speak to my mother like that. I can hear you all over the house."

"Adam . . ." Mama began, "Papa was not . . ."

"Why must you persistently defend him. The whole household is solely run for his comfort," words spilled from him, he could not have thought these things just then and there, they had to have been inside him for years, festering and growing. They were all so shocked that they stared at him, listening to his hatred of his father expressed in crippled statements of exaggerated accusation.

"You robbed my mother of her faith, you made her sneak out of the house to attend Mass as if she were attending a Witch's Sabbath, you ordered my uncle from the house, you forced us apart by making me go to school away from home."

Now there was another sound, the sound of mama's tears, and even these could not still his errant tongue, on and on he went, castigating his father, feeling inside himself no relief only anger. Then, finally, the last thrust, the final insult.

"Forcing her to have babies she does not want, nor is capable of having so that you can congratulate yourself on your virility and to hell with her."

"Get out! Get out of this house and never come back."

12

Adam heard his mother's cry of no, no, do not Josiah, do not, but not even for her would he stay, wildly he turned to leave colliding with his grandparents as he went. Grandfather turned from him in disgust, grandmother merely muttering that she had indeed known all along that he was no good, how could he be?

Now it was his father who had sought him out, his immaculate handsome father who had finally and irrevocably parted him from his mother.

"Well?" Adam asked tersely.

"Your mother was upset that you did not come to grandfather's funeral."

"Grandfather made it perfectly clear what he thought about me. I doubt that even in death his opinion changed, so why should I charge around to his funeral."

"Respect," Father said.

Adam would not be baited, nor would he answer. Josiah began to regret his mission; for himself he did not care if he never saw his son again, but she did. He had watched her become thinner, paler and melancholy, though she endeavoured to hide these feelings from him. She did not laugh anymore and he loved to hear her laugh!

"I think you should call and see your mother," Papa said at last.

"I do not ever want to step into your house again!" Adam retorted, going to rinse out one of his brushes in a small glass pot.

"Do you not care about your mother?"

"Unlike *you*, I love my Mother," he said.

Josiah sighed, there was no point in defending his own feelings for Sarah. Adam had long ago decided that his father could not possibly love her with the same passion as himself.

"Would you meet her somewhere?" Papa asked, at the same time going to stand by the door to prove to his son that he was now going to leave.

"All right, tell her I'll meet her on Friday at three o'clock in Piccadilly."

"You will turn up?"

"I never break *my* promises," Adam said.

Rosie came back much later to find Adam lying upon the bed, his arms behind his head staring up at the ceiling, watching the flickering shadows created by the well burned candle. It was cold now in the room, he had no fuel. Someone owed him money but until he was paid he had nothing.

She wondered if he had got some money from his father but dared not ask.

"I am not going to do any more painting tonight, he's bled the very inspiration from my veins."

She came and stood looking down at him.

"He's a handsome man, your father," she said.

"Women think so," he replied, "he's also very rich." He turned to look at her, his eyes looked black in the poor light. "He's also a bastard," Adam said.

Rosie sat beside him, looking at him. He was nice to look at too, but he did not have any money. He was as poor as she. Someone who knew someone who had worked in the office of his grandfather's lawyer, had told her that Adam had been left nothing. That at one time he had been left a considerable fortune but that old man Ayesthorpe had changed his will.

"Why do you hate him?" she asked. He did not reply and was still for so long a time that she feared she had gone too far, that he would send her away, but she was wrong, he raised himself, pulled her down beside him, sought her mouth and kissed her into submission.

14

"Of course I feel sorry for her, but then again I am certain she brings much of it upon herself, that boy always was so spoiled!"

"But given the circumstances," Elizabeth Grey murmured.

"Ah yes," Lucy whispered, "given the circumstances that he was there before . . ." they giggled.

William could hear them, though he pretended disinterest by looking out of the window. The new kitchen maid was there, industriously swilling down the marble steps. She was small and neat with dark curling hair and blue eyes. William liked small doll-like women. His own wife Elizabeth was considered attractive but he did not think her so. She was too tall and too large-boned for his taste, and she was fair. He did not find fairness appealing.

He listened to Lucy and Elizabeth gossiping, she liked to gossip, could happily spend hours picking holes in someone's character, no detail was too small for her not to be interested in it.

The match had been struck with money and breeding in mind, and since both had the former the latter had been of prime importance.

Elizabeth's father was a peer, a family that went beyond the Restoration, and although Elizabeth Northcote did not appeal to his senses he thought that fact of no criteria. Sensual pleasure could be had beyond marriage.

Neither was Elizabeth fond of the physical side of marriage, not that he had ever put himself out to encourage her. William was as selfish in his lovemaking as he was in all other matters.

However, she had provided him with a fine son Charles, and two fairly attractive daughters. After the birth of the last girl they had mutually agreed to come

15

together no more. Elizabeth had been honest about her distaste and he had been reasonable. All she asked was discretion, and he was anyway absolutely discreet, since he had been for some long time keeping a girl in a house near Rusholme.

He was though now tiring of the girl, and was avidly seeking fresh pastures. His eyes once more strayed to the new maid, she was very young, thirteen or fourteen but comely and she looked just a little like her.

"Although she is my sister-in-law and I truly love her, I must admit she is full of fault."

Ah, William thought, smiling a little as he saw the little servant empty the contents of her bucket into the rose beds rather than carry it around the back to the drain, they are talking about her!

Even today Sarah Ayesthorpe could stir his blood, whenever he saw her he experienced a feeling so strong that it was like nothing else. She was a matron, had a son who was turned twenty and a daughter of sixteen yet still she had the power to move him. Though they never spoke or passed the time of day, still now and again he would spy her in the streets. If she saw him she gave him a look of smouldering hatred that only increased his arousal. How he would have liked to drag her off somewhere, but unfortunately one could not do that to the wife of a prominent and respectable citizen of Manchester, not and get away scot free.

Socially their paths did not cross, though sometimes he would see her husband, but Joss Ayesthorpe never spoke to him, had not done so for many years. They would nod but that was all. Not that it really bothered William. He had his own set of friends, men of business bored him, he far preferred those who spent their days hunting and shooting.

"I heard a rumour," he drawled, "that your father left

16

Sarah's boy out of the will."

Lucy sniffed. "George says it is not right, but I cannot agree. My little Georgie works so hard at the factory, I'd have thought he would have been left half the business but Papa always was unpredictable. Josiah gets the business—all of it—which is most unfair. Of Papa's personal fortune Josiah and I receive a quarter then the rest is divided between George and Frank and Maureen. Mama of course was dealt with separately years ago, and I think I can safely say that Maureen and Adam won't benefit from anything she might leave."

"And Sarah?" William asked.

"Nothing for Sarah, which seems a shame but then Sarah will always do things her own way. I said to her countless times, don't spoil that boy, she never listened. I told her it was her duty to give up her religion but she would not. I mean how ridiculous she'd been without it for years, then she had to take it up just as if she had never lost it, embarrassing my brother with her awful Irish relations, and then there was that day she showed up the whole family, right in the middle of a demonstration of the working classes she was when the poor old Duke of Wellington came on the train to Liverpool Street Station, remember Peterloo indeed—who wants to, that's what I always say. No wonder Papa left her nothing. Poor Josiah, no one knows what he's had to suffer. If only he had married your sister, William," Lucy tool out a small lace handkerchief, she wiped away imaginary tears and sniffed loudly. Though why she felt the need to weep for his sister was a mystery to William, since the beautiful Arabella, with whom Joss Ayesthorpe had once been in love, had after being widowed from a first husband, married a duke three times her age, and having seen him into his grave had inherited vast estates in the southern shires and was currently something of a doyen of London Society.

William turned his attention once more to the little maid who was now going around to the side entrance. Small and neat. Yes, William, thought. I'll have her.

Two

"Mama," he said, and stooping he kissed her cheek. She was wearing a hat with a feather, it tickled his nose. She was in mourning as she seemed always to be these days. Black did not become her she was so dark with a complexion inclined to olive, but to him she was always beautiful. His lovely mama. Her of the dark crisply curling hair and violet eyes that flashed or were mysterious and sombre. They had been so close, so intimate, once upon a time they had had no secrets from each other. He had slept in her bed and smelt the delicious lavender scent that her skin gave off. They had played and run together, held one another and cried together.

When after four long years of a bitter marriage Papa had decided that he too loved her, Adam had felt himself being pushed out. Not by her, not by Mama but by his father; then it was he who slept in Mama's bed, who kissed her and was wont to touch her. Then finally he had sent him away to boarding-school. Adam could never forget that day, when the time came for him to leave. He had never imagined in a million years that his father would do that to him. That he would be taken from his mother's side. He had clung to her skirts and felt her arms go around him, and his father, that cold autocratic voice demanding that he behave like a man.

School had been detestable. He had hated every moment. Loathed the fagging, the punishment, the tears, the beatings, none of this he dared to tell her during the holidays, he wanted her to think him a success, wanted and needed her to be proud of him, living in

19

the optimistic dream world where Mama did not see the reports he brought for his father. Those reports that were poor and that frequently suggested that the boy might be better elsewhere. He was unaware of his mother's nightly pleading to her husband.

"Please let him come home, please, please if you love me let him come home."

"No. Go to sleep Sarah, I have to slave in that bloody mill, so he can learn to accept school."

Since his father had had a stroke Josiah had not, as he had done in the past, been able to travel the road. Not a glamourous job but one, he now realized, infinitely preferable to toiling away in the noisy mill and warehouse. In order to make things easier he had sold his Oldham factory and had bought a new one in the town, but his father's infirmities had meant that all the pressures that old man Ayesthorpe had taken on with relish had fallen onto Josiah's shoulders, and often he felt he was not up to them.

"You're thin," Mama said with Mama-like concern.

"I have always been thin."

"Do you eat?"

"I eat, I know that without food to sustain me I will become ill, and if I am ill I cannot work and if I cannot earn a copper I am destitute, so I eat."

"Do you earn?" Mama asked.

"I prostitute my art, Mama. I paint portraits of the ugly daughters of the lesser persons in town, and I make them prettier. It pleases them and I am neither so proud or so stupid that I do not lean on the Ayesthorpe name. Clerks and Ministers enjoy boasting that their adored child's portrait was painted by the grandson of Adam Ayesthorpe."

Mama put her hand through his arm, he had not chosen the most splendid of venues for the meeting, had

20

he thought more on the matter he might have suggested that they meet out in the countryside. It would have been pleasant to walk along lanes by rolling meadows, the day was fair and bright with a westerly wind, more like spring than winter.

"It's all right," Mama said when he had stated his regret at not thoroughly thinking about where they should meet. "We are together and that's all that matters. I'll take you to tea and buy you lots of sticky cakes. You used to so love sticky cakes. Adam, who is Rosie?"

He laughed and she stopped to pause and look up at him, puzzled and not a little concerned. He could well imagine what his father had said. In the old days he would have teased Mama, or perhaps have told her just a little lie to spare her feelings, but there was not the time anymore. They would have this couple of hours together and then who knew when, or even if, they would be allowed to meet again.

"She lives in the building and models for me."

"I see," Mama did not see, was uncertain and could not resist prying a little further. "You cannot afford to pay her very much, does she have other employment, or perhaps," she brightened, "she is married."

"I pay her what I can," Adam said, "she has a young child, a little girl, so she cannot work, well she could if she left little Dorothy with a minder, but the women who do that sort of thing, at least round where we live, aren't very reliable. There's a man who comes, a couple of times a week,' he pays her rent and gives her a little money."

Mama was silent and Adam felt himself redden. He was aware of her censure and even as it angered him he also understood it. Mama would make no such compromise.

21

"And the father of the child?"

"She was married, he worked in the pit. He was killed and so she lost everything."

Mama and a friend of hers had started a small school for children from poor families and, characteristically, she immediately offered a place for Dorothy so that Rosie could find respectable work.

He wished he had not told her so much, that he could now extricate himself from this conversation, he wanted to talk about himself and about her and not about Rosie who was all right but about whom he did not particularly care one way or the other. He and Rosie had a casual relationship based upon a mutual need, it was not even a friendship. Now he saw that he had to put an end to the conversation and that he must wound Mama a little.

"Rosie doesn't want respectable work, she likes her life as it is. It's easier and as to your school she doesn't like papes either."

Mama was silenced upon the matter, and if she felt rebuffed she did not show it to him, like Adam she felt their time together was too precious for them to spend too much time arguing about comparative strangers. She had wanted to know how deep his relationship was with the girl Josiah had described as a slut (it being Josiah's description she had not taken it too much to heart—in Josiah's eyes there were only two sorts of women) and Adam had to some extent satisfied that curiosity. He was not involved with the girl and that was all that mattered.

They took tea, she buying him all those things that he had loved to eat as a child, for Mama he had never become a man, he was still her much loved child. He could see this in the way she looked at him, her head a little to one side and her eyes bright with unshed tears. She was endeavouring to be pleasant and calm and reasonable but in the end she failed and said.

"Please come home, it will be all right. You can have the whole of the top floor to yourself. Please, *for me*?"

If she had asked him for the moon, or a bright little star he would have done his utmost to accomplish the task. He would try to give her anything she desired but he could not go home, could not endure to share his life with *that* man.

"You are so wrong about Papa, he is not what you think. He loves you, you are his son and to speak as you did to him hurt him beyond . . ."

"And what about his hurting you?" Adam asked, clenching his fists beneath the table, "and for no good reason."

"Your father has never willingly hurt me, not for many years. Oh he can be set in his ways, sometimes irritable and irritating," she smiled, "a little pompous and inclined to see things clearly marked, but it is because of these things that I love him. He would not be Josiah without these traits. 'It's these things inside him that make him do things, good things. To take up causes, to fight for free trade . . ."

"That is so he can improve his own lot," Adam snapped.

"Catholic emancipation," she said, trapping him. He could not gain from that since Josiah did not seek elected office. "Better conditions for workers. Men fight tooth and nail to work for him, especially since grandfather's death. They know they get a fair deal."

"I did not agree to see you in order to worship at the holy sepulchre of my father's impeccable character," Adam said unreasonably, spitefully but not regretfully. Mama bowed her head so that he could not read her expressions. That she loved his father he could never understand. His father had been forced to marry her by grandfather because she had been pregnant. Josiah had

23

never hidden the fact that he had been forced into the marriage, nor had he developed an overnight affection for his son. Ann, their housekeeper, had once been talking to old Hannah, who used to work for his grandparents, and from that conversation Adam had gleaned considerable information. Though he knew that it was not proper to listen, and more especially take in servants' conversations, he had been unable to resist their interpretations since both had been sympathetic towards Mama.

"How is Maureen?" He asked about his sister in an effort to restore a mood of amiability between them and Mama grasped it with both hands telling him of his sister who was going through an impossible stage and being as awkward with her Mother as it was possible to be without coming out in absolute rebellion.

Maureen he thought deserved a good hiding which made Mama laugh since her daughter was almost half Mama's size again, taking as she did after the Ayesthorpe women, being tall and nicely shaped.

Mama had lost three children and had had countless miscarriages. He could recall all those times she had had to stay in bed, pale and ill. Of the three children two had been born dead and a third survived only a fortnight. It had been a long time before he learned that it was his father who had brought her so close to death, the final fuel to the embers of his hatred.

"You don't understand me do you?" He said to his mother as he escorted her to the spot where their coachman had been instructed to collect her.

"Yes I do," she said, "more than you know. Will you see me again?"

He looked into her eyes, her eyelashes were long and dark, a fitting frame for her gentle eyes. She had to be thirty-five years old and yet at times she might have been

24

seventeen. All afternoon in the street, in the tea house, he had been aware of people looking at her, of respectable gentlemen raising their hats to her and workmen, carters and Irish labourers who were working on the streets, touching their forelocks. Of beggars coming before her, and street-sellers raising their hands to wave at her, everyone it seemed knew his mother, but how and from where he did not know.

"I'll see you once a month, on the second day of each month. I couldn't stand to see you more, to have to part with you."

"Oh Adam," she said, "I do love you."

"I know, Mama. See here's your coach, Good evening, Ernest, how are you?"

"Very well, Master Adam," Ernest said and despite Adam's assurance that it was all right, climbing down to open the door of the conveyance for Sarah, then standing aside until she was comfortable.

"Be good and be kind," she said to Adam, leaning out of the window and kissing his cheek. "God bless."

He watched until the coach was out of sight. Idiotically he was crying.

"What is your name?"

Startled the small girl turned to look up the long length of her master. Now and again she had spied him but naturally enough they had not spoken previously.

"Jane sir," she said, remembering as the plump not unfriendly cook had told her, to bob a curtsey should any of the family speak to her.

"Jane but not so plain, eh?"

She stood awkwardly looking up at him. Also she remembered that Mrs Phillips—who was the housekeeper—had told her that she must only speak when spoken to; that rule to also apply to all the other servants in the household. She was the lowliest of them all and must constantly remember this fact. Jane could not, therefore, sort out in her mind whether she was supposed to answer the master's remark, was it indeed a question or merely a statement?

For a moment he glanced over his shoulder to see if they were being observed, turning back quickly to the small girl who was still staring up at him, on the verge of trembling because she did not know what she should do. Close to she was not really very much like her. Her complexion was pale, her eyes a definite blue and though her hair curled naturally, from what he could see of it beneath her cap, it was not like jet but was darkest brown. However she was small and trim and pretty enough with her little snub nose and small well defined lips.

He put out a hand resting it on her shoulder, she started, her mouth parting, but unsure what to do, being utterly confused she stood straight as he slid his hand down over her bodice until he found the round hardness of a budding breast enjoying the hot flushes that stained her cheeks, the wetness that invaded her huge eyes.

"I'll come for you tonight," he said, then regretfully released his hold upon her. It was almost teatime and if he did not join his wife and family, servants would be sent to seek him. Elizabeth was extremely strict about the family sharing their meals together.

Cook looked up as the door was flung open by the little kitchen maid, the child was flushed and tearful and closing the door with her back fell against it sobbing in so distressed a manner cook forgot to utter an admonition, but wiping her flour-caked hands went across to the girl.

"Why whatever's up with you girl?"

"He . . . he," she began, then raising her arm up to her face to furiously wipe her nose upon her sleeve.

"He, he who?" Cook asked, not about to reprimand

the girl for her habit since it was one of her own.

"He touched my boozom, he said 'he'd come for me tonight. He was so to me, Missies, 'tis the truth.'"

"Sir William?" the cook asked.

"Aye, t'were him, an' I didn't know what to say."

"Well then, girl you've two choices, just two. Either you stay or you go."

"Stay or go, Missies?"

"Aye stay or go. If you stays then you gets him, if you goes you gets no character and no more housework, least not in a respectable household."

"Gets him, Missies, gets him? I don't know what you mean."

Cook tutted, then taking Jane's arm pulled her into the kitchen. Fortunately they were alone otherwise Cook would never have risked her own position by giving advice to a skinny little urchin from the dwellings who should anyhow know how to take care of herself. She gave the shivering little rabbit a drop of tea before speaking.

"You knows," she said at last, "how you gets babies," Jane nodded, "well that's what he's got in mind for you, only not the babies. So take your pick."

"But we isn't married. Me and Sir William, me brother said as you must be married before you get babies, he was most particular to tell me seeing as he was always getting Ellie with babies."

"Eh, the naïvete of the child," Cook muttered. "Just believe me, he'll have you in his bed quicker than it takes to break eggs. Course you might decide as that's more to your fancy than kitchen maiding is but . . ."

"I don't want him to touch me boozom no more," Jane said, on the verge of tears once more. "Can you tell her ladyship to tell him not to touch me?"

"Nay I cannot. Quite honestly all that's left for you to

27

do is to go home, and to go home right now."

Jane Marsden walked home from Levenshulme to Manchester. It was a few miles and it had begun to rain. Cook had not told anyone her secret but had given her some pie and a wedge of cake to take home as a peace offering. Jane did not think there would be much peace for her. Her brother and his wife had hoped to have wiped their hands of her, and a job in service was not to be walked out of.

A job in service was respectable work, better than her job as a loom cleaner in the factory. Not only that but there was no room for her anymore in the cellar of the dwelling where she had lived all her life. There was only Joe left now of her family and he had his own wife and children and now needed what little room they had. That was how come a reverend gentleman had found the position as kitchen maid for Jane, now she had lost that, and she was not sure that Joe would place much value on her virtue. Well she valued her self-respect and she felt quite certain that married or otherwise she would not allow any fellow to do to her what Joe did to Ellie sometimes at night.

It was dark when she reached the dwellings. She had her shawl up over her head and flitted through the grim shadows given off by the lamplight here and there, like a night imp. She ran the rest of the way, not wanting to get stopped by a nosey constable, or to be waylaid by drunken factory workers on their way home from the gin shop, but once inside the building she stood in the hallway to catch her breath and also to calm her nerves. She was at that minute more frightened of what Joe might say than by William Grey's fondling of her breast.

"Well then tell them and see if I care," so saying his cousin tossed her auburn curls and went to step ahead of him.

28

"It is not my intention to tell them about anything. I am not a spy," George Littlemoss Junior insisted. "I am merely counselling you in caution. Your father would not be pleased if he knew that you had been out walking unchaperoned with a man, and such a man!"

Truthfully Maureen was trembling a little inside. If cousin George had seen her who else might have seen her out walking alone with Charles Grey. Papa would be furious, and when Papa was angry it was frightening to her, who rarely witnessed his anger, and yet her meetings with Charles Grey held such an element of excitement she doubted that, in spite of the risks, she would be able to resist Charles's entreaties that they meet.

Maureen turned to look at George, there being hardly any difference in their height, they met eye on. She was an enchanting creature who never failed to cause blushes to invade his cheeks.

With her dark auburn hair and reddish brown eyes she was and was not similar to his mother, but she was certainly more like his mother than her own. He only hoped that Maureen would not go beyond plumpness as his own mother had done.

"I won't see him again, George," she lied, giving him what she hoped was a sincere and contrite smile. George was so dull but useful as an ally.

"I do not think you should, both your parents would be distressed. You know there has been bad feeling between them and the Greys for years."

Maureen did know, as did Charles but it was wrong for them to be expected to carry it on down into their generation, especially since they seemed drawn to one another.

Ever since they had met at Linda Barlow's party it was, she supposed, instant attraction, the meeting of eyes across the dance floor, the sort of thing that happened in all the romances which she avidly read, and

Charles was so handsome, easily the best looking young man in the whole of the town, next to her brother that was, but Adam did not count!

As she was so tall it was difficult for her to come across suitable young men; she was always made to feel their equal when she longed to feel small and in need of protection. Oh why had she grown so! Yet another reason for resentment against Mama who was so tiny Papa could lift her with one arm!

With Charles Grey no such problems existed, Charles Grey was six feet and broadly made, enabling her to feel doll-like instead of large and clumsy.

Her Aunt Lucy, with whom she had much more in common that she had with Mama, was her chaperone at this party, as she was for many of the functions her niece attended, since she was about more in the social scene than was Sarah, who was not fond of going out and about in society. It was better anyway because Aunt Lucy being lazy by nature was inclined to grant far greater leniency towards her niece than Sarah ever would, and if Charles Grey did seek out Maureen all to the good. Lucy liked her niece because she was so understanding and kind, and she would like the girl to make an advantageous match.

Josiah's feud with William Grey was utterly ridiculous, she herself was very friendly with all the Greys and could not understand Josiah's obdurate refusal to make friends; after all it was so childish just because William had once unintentionally been ungentlemanly to Sarah —and truthfully Lucy often though—who could blame him, Sarah's reputation was hardly spotless but then Josiah always was so very stuffy!

There they were then Charles Grey and Maureen Ayesthorpe dancing and talking together; how lovely the girl was Lucy thought, just as she herself had been at sixteen.

Ever since that night Maureen's head had been filled with Charles Grey. She had expected him to call but he had not done so realizing before she did that his call would be most unwelcome.

In misery she had gone to Aunt Lucy's in Fallowfield and lo and behold he was there! Being lavishly entertained by her aunt while she, Maureen, had practically starved herself as she pined longingly for a glimpse of him.

Aunt Lucy let them walk in the grounds of the house alone. They walked by the ornate lake and through the rose gardens. There was extensive parkland attached to the house and they could, therefore, wander at will for some considerable time.

Charles made her feel strange, elated and sad at one and the same time, her breasts tingled and she could not breath without effort when she met his eyes. She was tongue-tied and silly and could merely murmur only yes and no to all his conversation, so he would think her unintelligent and gauche. With all her other beaus she was tart and fiery, constantly sending them away with a sharp retort but with Charles she was an imbecile.

"Oh Aunt Lucy," she said after he had gone. "I feel so strange." And Aunt Lucy, her own dream of romance having been shattered on her wedding night, willingly encouraged Maureen to have her romance.

"Enjoy it," she said, "for I do assure you before marriage is the best time of all!"

Maureen even visited grandmother's house in Ardwick, though she never lingered long, grandmama was a spiteful old woman who constantly complained about Maureen's mother, and though the girl was not favourably disposed to Sarah she did think that grandmama's constant harangue was excessive. These visits anyway

31

were only an excuse to get away from her parents' house at Newton.

After leaving grandmama's she would meet Charles upon the Green, and here they would take their ease by sitting upon a bench near a spreading tree. It was here that Cousin George had spied her much to her chagrin, but she was certain that she had bought his silence by being charmingly contrite, at least for the moment.

"It's all so unfair," Charles Grey had complained "we are being punished for something that is not our fault. I know not the reason for your parent's animosity, do you?"

But Maureen did not and dare not question in case her secret be discovered.

"My father said that your father would have gained a knighthood but for your mother," Charles had told her. Her catholicism was an embarrassment as was her Irish connection. He did not mention out of delicacy the birth of Maureen's brother after only four months of marriage, but she was well aware of the fact. She had heard it often enough from grandmama, how Mama had tricked Papa into marriage by allowing him to be familiar with her, and consequentially finding herself with child. It was all a mystery to Maureen but she knew that she was expected to be disgusted with Mama, and in fact she was.

She saw quite clearly that Mama had spoiled Papa's life, that she had held him back and what was of more import, that the feud between her immediate family and the Greys' had quite a lot to do with Mama. Mama was it would seem about to ruin her happiness just as she had ruined Papa's. Resentment ran riot through every pore of her body.

"Put your feet up and let me put this shawl around your shoulders. There now, sip your tea."

32

"Oh Ann do not fuss so, I'm perfectly all right."

"No you're not, and don't tell me you're all right when I know perfectly well that you're not! I'm not an idiot to be fobbed off with excuses and if I don't fuss you I'd like to know who will."

Sarah smiled, sipped her tea and decided to say no more; if she wanted peace and quiet then telling Ann not to fuss her was the one way not to get it.

"How was he any road?" Ann asked before going from the room.

"Thin, so very thin."

"He always was thin, even as a lad. Don't go seeing things in that."

"No, I promise not to."

"Right then, have a good rest and I'll be up to get you dressed for when Mr Ayesthorpe comes home."

Josiah had, it seemed, overnight become Mr Ayesthorpe after years of being Master Josiah. We are growing old Sarah thought.

She was so very tired, and though she had intended to read, instead took refuge in sleep.

When Ann looked in on her later she saw her fast asleep and rather than wake her crept away. Let him see for himself, she thought, going downstairs. If she, Ann, knew what was wrong with his wife then there was no reason why he should not know. It was always the same, no one had to *mither* Josiah, everything had to be hushed up so that he could have his peace when he arrived home.

Sarah's father, old man Ogden as the servants called him, sneaked in to the house without a by your leave to anyone, as Ann said to old Hannah when she visited her, something's up with the old feller, or the old feller is up to something. He was always coming and going and walked about as if he carried a bag of secrets about with him. Eh well, it was nowt to do with her what old man

Ogden was about and she wasn't about to disturb Sarah's peace by telling her of her suspicions.

When Mr Ayesthorpe arrived home Ann did not bottle anything up and to his question as to where his wife was she said in bed sleeping. He turned and stared at her, his eyebrows rising as he repeated. "Sleeping?" in that fancy manner he had of speaking. Always did fancy himself a cut above everyone else did Joss Ayesthorpe. She had been with the family too long, knew all their business, had witnessed their ups and downs from the front row so she was now moving away from the realms of quiet respect to become as one of them, albeit in the role of super critic.

"Aye asleep, she has a rest most afternoons but today she's slept on, seeing as she saw young Adam and was . . ."

But Josiah had swept by her, and was running up the stairs two at a time. "Always did think himself better than anyone else and never was fit to lick her boots," she muttered going through to the kitchen.

"Oh!" she said struggling up out of the depths of sleep. Her eyes beneath slightly swollen so proving her not to have been merely taking an afternoon's nap. "I am sorry, I did ask Ann to call me."

"My dear, are you all right? Ann tells me you often take to your bed. You have never told me. What is it?"

He took her hand, so small and lost in his, her unpinned jet curls spread down over her white lawn underdress so that with her large bruise-coloured eyes she looked almost fifteen again. Fifteen and upon her bed offering herself to him.

"I am perfectly all right. You know how Ann does fuss so. I was just tired that's all. Please do not fret!"

"If you are sure?"

"Yes, yes, come let me get up, you must wish for

34

your supper."

"I can wait. You saw him?"

He questioned staring deeply into her eyes. She told him of her meeting with their son, although carefully omitting some of Adam's remarks regarding Josiah.

He listened silently while helping her into a dress of silk, black of course since they were still in mourning for his father, but it was becoming with its fitted waist and flowing skirts. Her dressmaker used no whalebone, she did not need it, nor a corset, with her tiny frame she was the favourite shape of the moment and needed no help (unlike, heaven forbid, his sister) to achieve it. When he had fastened the top most button he kissed her neck.

"So he won't come home," he said, after they had eaten and he was sipping his port and smoking a cigar.

The habit of smoking had come to him late, but now he enjoyed the fragrance and taste of an excellent cigar after his meal. It gave him a sense of well-being. Sarah as was usual took a glass of port with him; they did so only when alone, should they have guests Sarah would retire with the ladies and take tea.

She liked a drop of port though, and it amused him to indulge her. Once when he had started to smoke she had tried his cigar but that was not to her taste and she had choked upon it. That was what was so wonderful about her, she was not afraid to try. Life with Sarah since he had come to value her, less than twenty years ago, had never been dull or uneventful. He had thought their happy life would go on and on for ever but he had not bargained for his son. He could not understand him, could not touch him and he also realized something that was quite frightening, he did not like him very much.

He did not admit this to his son's mother, but he did confess a lack of understanding where his son was concerned.

35

"It's his Irishness," Sarah said, as if she had known this fact for many years. "The Celt in his soul. He can't help it."

"His Irishness? Where does he get his Irishness from?"

"My mother's side, the Donovans," she said, and as she spoke her eyes filled with misty tears. Any mention of her mother caused the tears to grow in her eyes but she had learned to control this tide of emotion admirably. Sadly he watched her struggle and win, when she looked at him again she smiled self-consciously.

Josiah had never met Sarah's Irish mother. Mary Kate had been killed when the local militia charged the crowds attending a political meeting on the 16th August 1819. Sarah had witnessed the incident and it had caused her to lose her memory. His father had found her frightened and ill and had taken her into his home to bring her up within the bosom of the family. It was six years before Sarah regained her memory, reliving the horrible day and discovering that it had been William Grey who had cut down her lovely mother in the prime of her life.

After much thought—they had— Josiah and Sarah— decided to keep this knowledge to themselves. To publicly state the facts would be of little use, since they doubted anything would be done to William Grey, who would anyway plead drunkenness as an excuse, as had many of the local men. Even should he be punished it would not bring Mary Kate back, and to comb over the past would upset Sarah's father whose heart had all but been broken over the incident, and who had then, at that time, started to settle down.

"So your poor mother is to be blamed for Adam's peculiar behaviour," Josiah suggested in an effort to help her.

"Not mammy particularly, but he is a bit like

mammy's brother, my Uncle Sean. You do remember Uncle Sean?" she teased.

Josiah indeed did remember her uncle. Sean would drink too much and when he was drunk he would either never stop singing or would become argumentative. Sober he was nice enough but his great switches of personality were not such that they would endear him to Josiah, who had had to see him off the premises on more than one occasion. Now and again he returned, was given money and then went upon his travels once more. However at fault Adam might be, he could not see his son as being in the least bit like Sarah's Uncle Sean, and told her so.

"It's a romantic sadness deep inside them. Dark, deep feelings, at least that is how I see it," she said gently.

"Do you have it?"

She shook her head, "No, it passed me by, but a little of it has gone into Adam. It fights with his reasonable Anglo-Saxon nature. You will compromise, he never can. He will not put up with things but will fight for his right—as he sees it—for self-expression. That's why latterly he did not get along with your father, only I dared not to explain it in those terms to him, he would have said it was nonsense. Perhaps it is, but that is how I measure my son. Two sides but following the romantic Celtic side of his nature."

"Come," he said, "come and sit upon my lap, let us hope that he takes it upon himself to throttle the Irishness out of his personality."

I do not think he ever will, Sarah said to herself, but she would not tell Josiah that. She did not think that Adam would ever come back to them, he would never chase away his dreams to such an extent that he would walk into factory or warehouse and take upon himself the reigns of Ayesthorpe business.

"I love you," he said as she nestled against him.

"I love you too," she lent against him, her head upon his chest, closed her eyes and slipped into an exhausted doze.

She was awake at first light; the bed was comfortable and the sheets were of fine cotton and not rags. Sleepily she sat up running her hands over her and feeling her clothing intact. She looked around at her surroundings; one upstairs room, untidy, a paint easel and there—there lying on the floor a blanket around him was—was Master Adam!

"Blooming heck!" she rasped, "what the blooming heck am I doing here?"

Gradually sense flooded her brain so that thankfully she lay back. Of course, Master Adam had found her in the hallway in tears.

It was easy to talk to Master Adam, there was something very comforting about his assurances that things were never so black you could not cope with them, and indeed make them better. It helped to make you strong, did adversity.

Instead of sending her down to Joe and Ellie he had taken her up to his room, and made her a cup of tea and given her a slice of bread with a lot of butter on it. She had never tasted butter before and never would she forget the flavour of it upon her tongue, the sweet creamy fullness of it.

Rather than have her face Joe that night he had then offered her his bed. "I'll be painting," he said, "and I'll try and sort something out for you in the morning. I won't promise but trust me to think it over."

The child's tale of woe had touched him deeply, and that was all she was, a child, and yet a grown man sought to basely use her. It made him feel sick and angry. It was not right that men could abuse children and not face any punishment. How would William Grey like it, Adam had wondered, if someone were to put their hands on his daughters. Doubtless he would be up in arms, it was not unlikely that he would have the would-be seducer flogged yet he could do such a thing to a child whose only recourse was to run away, who because she was poor, was punished whichever way she turned. I'd like to kick his teeth in, Adam muttered and then swore beneath his breath because in his anger he had used too much vermilion.

He had a little bread and butter and some tea left so made Jane something to eat and drink the following morning. Then they would go out because he thought he might be able to find her a place.

She washed their used dishes in the little bowl of water Adam had previously brought for her to wash in, while she waited for him to fill the container with fresh water from the pump out in the court. Then, having finished before he returned, she wandered around taking a long and serious look at his paintings.

When he finally arrived back she was looking, with severity at the nude study he had recently done of Rosie. It was not for sale but he had done it because he liked Rosie's body, enjoyed to look at her and thought that such beauty—which could not last forever—should be captured on canvas.

Jane turned as he entered the room, gave him a reproving look then thinking better of it said: "I'll bet Sir William would want to touch her boozoms."

Adam laughed, it was the first time in a long while that he had had the urge to really let himself go.

"Do you know Jane, you are a survivor. You are not only going to overcome any adversity that comes your way, but you are going to prosper!"

Three

"And if we want trade and prosperity all round we must be free from governmental restriction."

Josiah sat down to rapturous applause feeling inside himself a sense of elation, the adrenalin was gushing through his system filling him with so much energy that it was not difficult for his companions to persuade him to take advantage of all that London had to offer.

He had at first been surprised that John Bright had asked him to speak at an Anti-Corn League Meeting in his place, and then as he had discussed it with Sarah—to whom he took all this thoughts—he had felt flattered, a rare emotion for Josiah.

Sarah had advised him to accept, he was capable of giving a sincere speech upon the matter and with his concise manner able to present a reasoned argument.

He was quite at home in London. He had travelled extensively as a young man selling Ayesthorpe velvet and his lack of accent enabled him to move about society unself-consciously. His companions however were somewhat at a loss, their harsh vowelled Manchester accents and bluff manners becoming harsher and bluffer as they sought to prove that they did not care that smart Londoners looked down upon them as dull provincials.

After dinner they went into a gambling casino losing more than they could probably afford but determined not to lose face. Josiah did not gamble, gambling held no excitement for him so he lounged with a glass of brandy and a cigar in a comfortable armchair, watching his acquaintances with a mixture of irritation and amusement.

His workers were going to have to go on short time. Quite a lot of manufacturers had shut down completely until trade picked up, throwing their workers into the hands of the Poor Law Commissioners, which was something many were reluctant to bother with. They would use their savings or the pawn shop and only seek charity when these sources had been used. They were terrified of the workhouse, the final degradation, the splitting up of the family, father to one house, mother to another and children yet to another.

To Josiah his workers, rightly or wrongly, were part of his family, he was responsible for their well-being, he could not, would not lock them out so that he could make a better profit. His brother-in-law who liked to keep a watchful eye on the firm now that his son was employed there, had called him a fool. "Shut down man, they'll get by, the working class always does. They breed like vermin."

But Josiah could not agree, and neither did Sarah, whom he knew would be prepared to sell their home and to move to somewhere smaller rather than shut out the workers. However, it would not come to that. He would not let it. On short time he could carry on comfortably, and short time had to be better than no time at all!

"Eh, Joss," John Roughlee approached him. "I was talking to one of them flunkeys and he's told us about a house and we was . . ."

"No," Josiah said sharply, and then with a smile to soften his refusal. "You all go ahead, but I shall have an early night."

They went. He remembered his father always going on about fools and their money soon being parted. He still was not tired but he did not want to spend his energies at a brothel. He hadn't seen the inside of one of those places for about twenty odd years, not since he had fallen

41

in love with his wife.

He had another brandy and cigar, stood and walked slowly around the casino, admiring its sumptuous elegance, the dark red velvet hangings, not Ayesthorpe velvet he mentally noted. The deep red piled carpets and the glittering chandeliers. The women bedecked with precious jewels and furs and yet half a mile away people were living in hovels, huddling beneath old sacks to keep warm because they had no money to buy the coal that their social equals dug from the ground.

"Josiah," the voice refined and husky, the perfume richly exotic. He turned and looked into faintly slanting pale blue eyes, a tiny delicately moulded face surrounded by elaborately arranged pale hair.

"You!" he said, and then remembering his manners, "I'm afraid I don't know how to address a duchess, or is it Your Grace?"

She laughed, that gentle tinkling laugh that had teased him to distraction as a young man.

"Arabella to you, Josiah. What on earth are *you* doing *here*?"

Briefly he explained his reasons for being in London, all the time he was speaking noting that she was still quite lovely. There were tiny wrinkles at the corners of her eyes but even these were not unattractive, she was still that lovely Arabella Grey, slim and delicate in appearance, although it would seem that her fragility had nothing to do with her constitution.

As he was explaining why he was in London he noticed her smile and her "Oh Josiah, how middle class you have become and I thought you to be a Bohemian artist!" was wounding. However, he did not retaliate or offer a defence, besides he no longer cared what Arabella Grey thought about him.

"The last time I saw you you were beating my brother

42

with a horsewhip, such a cavalier, defending your wife's honour. How is your wife by the way, Sarah isn't it?"

She knew very well that his wife was called Sarah so he did not bother to confirm or deny his question.

A young man came up to her with every intention of taking her away with him, it was obvious by his attitude that he was her escort, but Arabella dismissed him telling him to leave her alone while she talked to someone from home. There was no one quite so cruel as Arabella when she wanted to be, she would dismiss someone only seconds after making them welcome. He could sympathize with the young man because in his own youth he had suffered greatly from very similar treatment when he had been in love with her.

"It's all right, Arabella, I am just about to leave," he said. Her arm came out, her hand the fingers of which were long and pale and white, curled around his arm.

"Oh no, Josiah, I cannot let you run away we have so much to talk about."

"We have nothing to talk about," he said, "Good-night."

Once back at his hotel he undressed and put on a robe, then after carefully hanging up his clothes, he took up pen and ink and began to work out the economic measures that had to be taken because of the poor state of trade. He was half way through it and totally involved when someone's knocking upon the door of his suite broke his concentration. He flung down the pen in rare bad temper and allowed himself the savage pleasure of using a vicious curse, something he rarely did.

He expected his revelling companions, eager to regale him with their adventures and was ready, words formed in his mind, to tell them what they could do with themselves. But it was not them; it was Arabella.

He stared at her unable to comprehend her sudden

appearance. The hood of her ermine-trimmed velvet evening cloak fell back, showing the full golden softness of her hair.

"You ran away from me Josiah," she said.

"I . . . I, no I didn't really, it's just that I had so much work to do." He was confused, unsure what to say or do.

"May I come in, or must we talk in this drafty corridor?"

Standing back he let her precede him into the rooms. Her eyes were as bright and shiny as the diamonds in her hair and hanging from her ears. To his greater consternation she undid her cloak and as though it were the cheapest rag in the world, cast it carelessly aside.

Her gown was of pale blue watersilk, it was cut low over her bosom, its skirt falling widely from her slender waist.

"What do you want?" he asked at length. She laughed, walking toward him, he was still standing by the door, his back pressed against the panels as if ready to throw himself through it.

"Champagne," she said, "yes, Josiah, let us have some champagne, do you know Madame Pompadour always maintained it was the one drink that a woman might take and still be beautiful the next day."

"Arabella, I do not wish to be rude but I have had an extremely tiring day and . . ."

"Oh Josiah, can you not be gallant. You used always to be *so* gallant, waiting upon me, endeavouring to please. That can sometimes be so tiresome."

She was close to him, the scent of her was in his nostrils, crawling over him, clinging to his robe.

"You're very lovely," he said, "but spoilt and selfish."

Her eyes glowed, her lips parting.

"Don't stop," she said, "What else am I?"

He saw it all, after all these years, the answer to the

44

riddle of Arabella Grey. What she had wanted and why he had in his youth failed to capture her.

He was angry, angry with himself, with the vagaries of life, but most of all with Arabella.

"You're a bitch, and I do not entertain bitches in my room."

"I *didn't* do nothing with no vase," Jane declared with a sniff, facing Letitia across the room, bewildered at the accusation that she had stolen one of Mrs Ayesthorpe's precious vases; everyone knew she was as honest as the day was long. Jane Masden had never taken anything that did not belong to her in all her life, and it was anyway not up to any hoity-toity ladies' maid to say she had.

"Now, now," Ann, the housekeeper said, "You're new here and have come from a bad experience, perhaps you broke the vase and are afraid to speak up."

"No, T'i'nt so. I never did break no vase, an' if I had broke a vase I would've told Missies. A'nt she bin teaching me to sew, don't she talk to me, in't she kind, she would understand if I told her I broke her vase, but I 'aven't, may God strike me as I stand if I tell a lie."

"She loved that vase," Letitia said, "and especially asked for it."

"Well you'll have to tell her it's gone missing. If Jane swears she hasn't seen it, broken it or taken it then that's good enough for me."

Jane looked up at the elderly housekeeper, those were the first kind words she had had from her since Master Adam had brought her to his mother's house.

A place—albeit one quite lowly—had been found for the girl and, for the first time in all her life she had her own room, tiny it might be, but it was all her own. Mrs Ayesthorpe had instructed that Jane be trained by Ann and she herself would teach the girl to sew.

Jane adored her new mistress, enjoyed making the black-leaded kitchen range shine so that it would be pleasant for her to look upon, kept the fireplace in the lounge and parlour immaculately clean, always making sure there was coal aplenty for her mistress. Liked to polish the furniture so that it glowed so brightly that Mrs Ayesthorpe actually paused to admire her handiwork.

Never would Jane be able to thank Master Adam enough for fetching her to his mother's house. God was good, she decided, He had made her have a bad experience so that she would know how to really appreciate a good place.

"One dozen red roses," Ann muttered to the cook— Jane strained her ears while polishing the silver, any detail about her adored mistress was never too small for the girl to store and savour.

"Well he's been away," cook replied.

"Aye, so what's he been up to that he has to send red roses to his wife. When a man does summat like that it makes me think he's been up to no good.

Jane had only glimpsed her mistress's husband once. He was tall and slim and fair like his son, and quite as nice-looking although he had to be ever so old.

At that moment, someone knocked at the back door. Ann being the nearest opened it and let in the collector from the burial club who had come for the servants' contributions. Jane now having steady employment had taken over paying for her own; the greatest fear she had in common with the great majority of people was in not having enough money to pay for their funerals, dreading with real fear to fall behind with their weekly payments and so go to rest in a pauper's grave.

"Mrs Ayesthorpe said as you weren't to take any money from her father, that she'd pay for his funeral."

"Aye I know, she says one thing but he says another.

He catches me at the gate and makes me take his money, so what am I to do?" The collector explained.

"He's a stubborn old beggar right enough," Ann retorted, "Well I'm not going to mither her about it. I'll say nowt and to hell with him."

The bell rang in the kitchen, two rings, that was the call for Jane. She stood so quickly she almost knocked over the silver in her rush to wash her hands.

"Steady on," Ann said, then with a smile. "Don't be feared, Jinny Marsden, she won't say nowt about the vase. I know her, I know'd her since she were a little girl just like you."

Mrs Ayesthorpe was in the library, arranging the red roses that Mr Ayesthorpe had sent because he had been up to summat; exactly what up to summat was she not quite certain, all she hoped was that it was not anything that knowledge of would hurt Mrs Ayesthorpe."

"Jane," she said with a smile, "Come—come," she indicated that Jane should go towards the table where she was arranging the roses. On reaching the spot she heard the rustle of newspaper and saw that Mrs Ayesthorpe was not alone, that Mr Ayesthorpe was seated in the armchair with a copy of the *Manchester Guardian*. This he lowered to peer over its rim at her, causing her cheeks to flush as his very blue eyes met hers; it seemed an eternity that he looked at her, then without saying a word he lifted the paper once more.

"It's your day off tomorrow and I believe you will be visiting your brother and his wife."

"Yes, Madam."

"I've asked Ann to give you a little tea and a pie and a few odds and ends for them but I wonder if you would do me a special favour."

"Yes Madam, anything!"

Mrs Ayesthorpe smiled. "Would you take a note to

47

my son for me, and also a basket for him. Would it be too much trouble?''

A tut-tutting came from behind the newspaper. Sarah turned looked in the direction of the newspaper, frowned then looked back to the waiting girl who was assuring her that it was no trouble.

She had not closed the door when she heard Mr Ayesthorpe reprimand his wife for sending a basket to their son. Jane made her mind up that she did not like Mr Ayesthorpe, whether he sent roses to his wife or whether he did not.

Much to Jane's surprise Ernest who had business in town had been instructed to take her in the coach as she had two baskets to carry, and the walk from Newton to town would be uncomfortable for her.

Ernest was not at all pleased with this state of affairs, he was not in service in order to drive kitchen maids about the place, and showed his disgust by telling Jane to alight at the top of Newton Lane, rather than take her nearer to the dwellings. Not that Jane took offence, she had been too thrilled with the coach ride to allow Ernest's churlishness to spoil her pleasure.

With a basket over each arm and a warm shawl about her head and shoulders she took her ease walking along Oldham Street, and looking in at the tiny shops. It was a cool day but sunny and pleasant and inside she felt a rush of well-being. She knew it would be awful at her brothers, dark and grim and Ellie was cross because another baby was growing inside her and Joe was on short time. Joe would set about calling the Ayesthorpes and muttering words of revolution and about how unfair life was, and why did she not bring more, so that she was not eager to reach the dwellings and so sauntered and went the long way round.

She was at the top of Market Street Lane when she

became aware of someone's walking beside her. Immediately her chin shot high in the air, her expression one of disdain and her steps moving quickly; much to her chagrin his steps increased in time with her own.

"And where are you off to at such speed, *fach*," his voice was high and musical and by his accent proved that he was from strange parts. Curiously though not slowing her pace, she glanced at him. He was not very tall but had curly black hair and laughing blue eyes, though his clothes were of the poor workman and instead of a collar he wore a red neckerchief about his throat, altogether there was something bright and dashing about him.

"It's got nowt to do with you," she said sharply.

"No I suppose not, but I was just being friendly."

"What you following me for?" she asked, but slowing her pace. He did likewise, walking along side her, hands behind his back.

"Never saw one so pretty," he said a twinkle in his eyes, "clogs and a shawl and two little baskets, like a picture you are."

"Hmf," she said, but feeling delighted inside. No one—apart from Sir William—had admired her before. "You talk funny, where you from?"

She was too close to the dwellings now, they hovered before her eyes, a cluster of warrens of which she was unaccountably ashamed, so she now paused, showing great interest in a pawnbroker's window.

"From Wales," he said, "I came to work in the factory, there's no work at home. Went to Liverpool first and almost joined the navy."

"Why din't you?"

"Someone mentioned Manchester and how busy it was in the factories and the mills so I thought I'd come see first."

"Found a job did you?"

"Yes. It does not pay so much but it's a job and I am learning all the while."

She felt it might be impertinent to enquire from him further and so said that she must go as her sister-in-law would be looking out for her. He did not detain her further but stood leaning against the door of the pawn-broker's, hands in his trouser pockets, a roguish air about him.

Before turning into the small alleyway that led to her brother's building she turned. He was still there watching her, with a toss of her head she turned and ran, not stopping until she reached their Joe's.

The day spent with her brother and his wife and family was worse than ever and the only break came when she had to take Master Adam's basket up to him. However, she did not linger too long for it was obvious that he was most anxious to read the letter his mother had sent.

Once downstairs in the cellar depression began to roll over her in an ever-thickening pall. It was dank and dark in their two rooms, the light of day filtered through the small grid at street level but so did more odious things, but these her natural stoicism would have made tolerable, what was intolerable though was Joe and his constant harangue of the Ayesthorpes. Their wealth, his poverty. Why had she not stolen more food than what was allowed to her, or taken some knick-knack that would not be missed from its place amongst a clutter of paraphernalia that he was sure people like the Ayesthorpes collected.

His bitterness would not be appeased, his state was too pitiable Jane saw, he was trapped like so many more by the circumstances of trade. However, were trade better Jane doubted very much that her brother would raise himself for not only did he lack a flair of ambition, he was too fond of appeasing his senses, whether by using his

50

wife or visiting the gin shop too frequently.

"You should 'ave stayed with the Greys," Joe stated at last.

"But our Joe, I did tell you what Cookie said . . ."

"So! All the better you'd 'ave got more money for less work!"

Jane felt disgusted and the wail of Joe's youngest child seemed like censure to all of them. Ellie fearful that Joe may have alienated his sister, who quite willingly handed over all her wages, apart from threepence, to her brother, began to placate Jane, stressing that Joe had not meant what he said. Joe said nothing. The babies crying and the stink from the street outside finally made Jane determined to leave. She would bring them their basket and her wages, but no more would she spend her only day off sitting with them in their horrid apartments.

It was time that the seedling now fully grown set off elsewhere, and her roots she was certain would never grow and multiply in this den. She would demand more from life, demand it and take it!

So without further ado she made to leave, kissed the pale and sickly infants, brushed Ellie's tired cheek with her lips and merely told Joe that she would be off. He was sitting on an old tea chest, hands limply hanging between his knees. He knew he had gone too far, but did not know how to extricate himself. Certainly he would not, could not say he was sorry, that would mean losing face, and if Ellie dared to say anything about his behaviour she'd get a good hiding.

Ellie sensing his violent mood said nothing. She had had enough beatings in the past to be able to accurately gauge when and when not to offer up criticism.

Using his sister's ingratitude as an excuse he later made his way to the gin shop on the corner, and Ellie only hoped it did not take all of the money Jane had left to get him drunk.

It was still light and her leaving her brothers earlier gave Jane more time to herself. She thought she would walk to the very boundaries of the town where verdant meadows fell away endlessly and where it was sweet and pleasant to stroll. She had never before known idleness and was uncertain how to use it, feeling somewhat guilty.

On her next day off she would bring a little sewing with her, and if it was fine she would sit in a meadow practising, if it was not fine she could go back to the Ayesthorpes and sit in her room—her lovely room with the bright patchwork quilt she so loved—perhaps she could even learn to read. Oh, the possibilities she saw were endless.

He was still there! Lounging by the pawnshop and now as she came into view straightening and giving her a broad smile as if he had known her all his life. He was cheeky was that Welsher!

Jane did not return his smile, though she wanted to. She was uncertain what to do, since no man had chased after her before, and this Welsher was chasing after her that was certain because he now joined his step to hers.

"Rushing away again!" he said. She liked the soft lilt in his voice, it was musical and gentle.

"Haven't you any work," she said at last.

"Not today. Last night there was a breakdown, I was working 'till turned three o'clock and my master gave me a day off, is it."

"Is it!" she teased.

The Welsher continued to walk beside her. It seemed that he had decided to attach himself to her whether she wanted his company or not. Fortunately for him she wanted his company, and so she slowed her pace and they walked to the corner of Newton Lane chatting. Because she did not know him she changed her mind

52

about going to Chorton-on-Medlock and beyond. However when they arrived at Newton Lane she paused upon the corner.

"My name is Richard Jones," he said. "I'm from Rhyl and I am the middle son of three. What's your name?"

"Jane Marsden," she said and then in an attempt to prove herself above him in station she said. "and I am in service."

His eyes laughed at her. "I am my own man."

"Humph, that's what you say, but you still have to work for a master."

"Not for always. I am ambitious."

"Good for you."

He ignored her sarcasm. "'I have good lodgings with a lady in Ancoats, she's very kind. Would you come to tea?"

"Would I come to tea? To your house? Indeed I wouldn't. I've told you, I'm no factory girl. I am in service and my mistress wouldn't like me taking no tea with no stranger."

"I won't always be a stranger to you, *fach*. You and me has some courting to do."

"You what?" Jane cried, feeling her cheeks flood with colour.

"You'll do me, Jane Marsden, my mind is made up, so when can we start into the courting properly, or will you ask your mistress first?"

"Darling," he had not heard. He was at his desk studying facts and figures. Now was not the time, but if not now when? She had put this conversation off for too long and it was not something that could be shelved indefinitely. She had wanted to tell him before he left for London but yet again she had felt the time not to be right.

"Joss."

He looked up vaguely and then with a guilty smile. They had long ago made a pact that their evenings together would be shared without the encumbrance of factory and warehouse, and ever since dinner at six, he had been working out a solution to his seemingly never-ending problems.

"I am sorry, sweetheart."

"No, it is not for that reason that I disturbed you. I have to talk to you."

"Oh, then all else may go hang."

He stood, flexed his shoulders, then after pausing a moment made to join her upon the settee where she had been quietly embroidering.

Her feelings when she looked at him erupted violently; they always did, always had. His long lean body, golden hair and finely drawn countenance had never ceased to please her, or to drive her thoughts winging from her mind so that she could think only of his kisses, his lovemaking, of being close to him. Never would a day pass by that she would not be grateful to have Josiah's love, something she had thought would never be hers.

He sat beside her. She took up his hand and threaded her short stubby fingers through his long slender ones.

"It appears that I am going to have a child," she said.

His groan was agony-filled and in shame he buried his head in her lap. His hand torturing the fine silk of her gown, grasping it and pulled it as though he were in pain.

"I am sorry," he said, "I am so sorry my darling."

"Do not be, it will be all right."

"But Doctor Hardcastle said . . ."

"Oh, he is old-fashioned. I saw the new doctor—that young Scotsman who has recently come to town—and he said if I rest, if I take care and do not worry about anything."

He moved his head to the centre of her chest, resting

his ear against her heart, hearing its steady calm beat.

"That's why you've taken to your bed of the afternoon. Oh Sarah, Sarah . . ."

Calmly she put her hand amidst his undulating golden hair, stroking it gently. "You have lots of silver hair now," she said, "are you going to be white-haired like your father, I wonder."

"Damn my hair," he said, "I am a careless selfish brute."

"Not at all. I thought it would be all right, but I was wrong. I am just as much to blame. Come, do not distress me with this self-torment."

"You must do nothing," he said, "nor must you be worried. I will instruct the servants . . ."

"Ann has probably done so. She guessed, she knows me so well and is aware of all the little things that affect me when I am starting a baby."

"Unlike me! God, how insensitive you must think me."

"You have been worried, Joss, and I did not want you to know and hid my secret well, and now," she smiled, "now that I have confessed I feel much better so we shall have a toast."

She went to stand to attend to their drinks but he settled her back and went to the drinks cabinet himself, pouring her her favourite port and a brandy for himself and took up himself a cheerfulness that he was far from feeling.

Sarah should not have any more children. Doctor Hardcastle was old and fussy and he had not taken to many of the new ideas but one thing was certain, he had been Sarah's doctor since she had first come to the Ayesthorpes with her lost memory. He had seen her and helped her through many trials and tribulations connected with her illness, and her various pregnancies, and if he had said Sarah should not have another child then he had to be speaking with great knowledge. Doctor Hardcastle knew Sarah's constitution inside out and he did not make such statements for the fun of them.

He had been so careful, so scrupulous since Sarah had vetoed the idea of their having separate rooms, and indeed as he had thought not coming together as man and wife. Perhaps his complacency had been the flaw in the arrangement, his congratulations upon his self-control, but that self-control had come undone one night and now there were to be dire consequences.

Elizabeth looked at her son admiringly. He was well worth the suffering she had had to endure, both in order to conceive him and to give birth to him. She quite liked her daughters but she loved Charles. Charles was her first born.

Though William had planted him to grow inside her, he had none of his father's flaws. William would have been amazed had he known that his wife knew *all* about him. Knew about the little whore in Rusholme, knew that he was obsessed by Sarah Ayesthorpe, even knew why the new maid had left so quickly. No detail about her husband was too small that Elizabeth did not write it down. It was her protection against him. Life was most pleasant now, she had freedom from William's advances, a sufficient allowance to comfortably amuse herself and good friends. However, should these things change then she had evidence of her husband's unsavoury conduct, and she would not hesitate to use it, either to his face or behind his back. Her family would not countenance William's behaviour. However, perhaps it would never be necessary.

"I have been hearing things, Charles. Things that have displeased me."

"Oh?" he said, though carefully. He always saw his mother as a spider, he did not trust her and nor much to his inner guilt did he like her very much. There was that about her he could not love, a coldness that came from her like a chilling wind. He took his tea and waited, though the quickening thud of his heart and the colour that ran into his cheeks made mock of his calmness.

"I understand you have been secretly meeting a young lady—an unsuitable young lady."

"Unsuitable?"

"Unsuitable, Charles."

"In what way is Miss Ayesthorpe unsuitable. I am right in assuming that you are referring to Miss Ayesthorpe?"

"You are," his mother smiled, "and before I give my reasons why I consider her unsuitable, I will just ask whether her own family knows of and approves this budding friendship."

He blushed, then shook his head.

"Quite," his mother said. "They would no more approve than your father and I. Though they do have less reason it must be said."

"What is wrong with Maureen, she is excellently brought up and . . ."

"Excellently brought up!" Mother said sarcastically, "yet she meets you in secret, without a chaperone, come now, a mill girl would have more sense."

Charles shifted on his seat, it was regretful but true. Maureen was indiscreet, though he implored her to meet him he had to admit that no other girl in his circle would do so, not that this had dampened his ardour any, if anything it had increased it. He could not see enough of her. Their secret meetings had increased to such an extent that they were seeing each other every day and they had obviously become indiscreet if his mother had heard about them.

His father joined them then and so the conversation was made up of banalities, he imagined that, for that day at least, the subject had been dropped. However, to his distress this was not to be.

Lady Elizabeth left him alone with her husband, having primed Sir William upon the matter, and he now gently castigated his son for becoming involved in a misalliance.

"I cannot understand what is so wrong with the Ayesthorpe's since I have been led to believe that Aunt Arabella was once considering marriage to Maureen's father."

"That is so, but Josiah Ayesthorpe is only her father. It isn't he we object to, but her mother."

Charles met his father's gaze steadily.

"Granted the girl is half Ayesthorpe, but what of that other side. I have told you about her mother, how she has held her husband back from greater things. It will take generations before people forget that she was their mother. I mean who is she? Where does she come from? Some shanty. She's Irish, she's a Roman Catholic and she was careless with her virtue."

As Charles did not know about his own father's private life he did not see anything hypocritical in his words, more they distressed him because it was true that Maureen's mother was a giant stumbling block.

"Extricate yourself now before she attempts to ensnare you as her mother ensnared her father." Sir William's eyes gleamed as he saw his son's blushes; at seventeen he should not be subject to flushing cheeks. Sir William would have liked to take his son out to some sumptuous establishment in order that he could learn how to be a man, but he knew his wife would forbid such a trip, even should he do so secretly he felt she might find

58

out and did not wish the peace of his life to be disturbed by a scene which could have far-reaching consequences.

"You have not gone too far in this affair, have you?"

"Good Lord, Father, of course not. What do you imagine Miss Ayesthorpe is?"

"Her mother's daughter I shouldn't wonder. However, that is by the by. Nothing can come of it, marriage is out of the question. We marry upwards Charles, not downwards. That has always been the way of our family. It is so easy to gather dirt from the gutter."

Charles stood, he was miserable and confused. He was meeting Maureen this afternoon on the Green. What would he say—what could he say?

"Find yourself a little actress to dally with," his father murmured, "they only expect presents."

With that he left his son, going now out to the waiting groom who had been saddling his horse. He would ride over to Rusholme, his interview with his son had left him in need of a diversion.

When he arrived back for supper the household was in a flurry of excitement with servants dashing about and great portmanteaus being carried up the stairs.

He came upon his wife who with cheeks of dark rose, as if cross about something, was giving orders to cook.

"What is it?" William asked pleasantly relaxed from his sojourn with his mistress. His wife saw it in his eyes, and knew the reason.

"Your sister," she snapped, "has just arrived. No word, no previous warning, she just sweeps in for an indefinite stay, typically inconsiderate."

"Arabella?" William questioned, "what does she want in Manchester. She loathes Manchester!"

"It is all a question of genius; some have it, and some do not. Then there is flair, and something in the soul, no?

59

My dear Mr Ayesthorpe I am delighted to be able to tell you that you have all three and in enormous proportions."

Adam stood his arms folded across his chest, his features set, his expression unemotional, no excitement or pleasure had taken root, there was a void, a nothingness.

The small man wandered the room gazing enraptured at the paintings, taking first one to the window and then another.

"This—the curve of her breast, these eyes that long for love, this child here—he asks, please feed me, and here, this river it asks, what have you done to me? They speak, they live!"

Adam said nothing. He had not invited the man to view his paintings, the man had invited himself in after presenting with aplomb his card, which was meant to impress, but Adam was not impressed, and *that* impressed Mr Sangster.

As a renowned and respected art dealer and critic he was sought by artists. By one of those rare twists of fate he had been dining at his club. It was not the best club in London, as far as members went, but since Mr Sangster had antecedents of a dubious religious persuasion the better clubs—even though he was successful in his sphere—were not open to him. However, he liked his club, the food was good and the atmosphere fairly convivial although some of the manufacturing classes he met there could be more boisterous than his taste appreciated.

One of these was a man who made parts for textile machinery. The man had begun on the factory floor and by guts, determination, and not a little luck had risen to own his own small firm. A man to be admired but one who had neither the time or the inclination to polish off the rougher edges of his personality. Sangster's taciturnity appealed to the fellow since he merely listened and said nothing and because of a rare envy of the other man's sophisticated elegance, Higgins began to boast of his latest acquisition, a painting, cheap, from the grandson of old man Ayesthorpe.

Sangster had been moved to chuckle, was then old man Ayesthorpe more important than the artist, his grandson.

"Of course," declared Higgins, "I well remember old man Ayesthorpe, what a man of business, what a genius, he knew how to make brass he did. Come up from a weaving cottage did old man Ayesthorpe," the man laughed, over loudly, "he was my inspiration if you like. He didn't bother about nowt, didn't care what anyone said about him, and there's his grandson living in the dwellings by the Irwell, painting pictures for a living and not making much at it. In a way it's good in't it, I mean my buying Ayesthorpe's grandson's pictures, in a way it's like me supporting him in't it?"

Curious Sangster had expressed a wish to see the painting. Old man Ayesthorpe he gathered had not an artistic bone in his body, so how badly did the grandson paint. Higgins invited Sangster to see it any time, and so the next time he had been in Manchester, Sangster had called to view it.

His reaction had confounded the manufacturer, he would never have envisaged him liking the painting, his liking of it had nothing to do with art appreciation—was it then art? Higgins would never know.

Now Sangster was confronted by more paintings, each one with something separate to say. He was overawed! Like Aladdin in his wondrous cave he could not stop lifting and studying and carrying them into the ever-diminishing light.

Finally he came upon the last. The light was failing fast

and Adam Ayesthorpe made no attempt to fetch candles. His disinterest was to Sangster, who was frequently beleaguered by artists, attractive, the more so because he read the sincerity in it. The young man painted because he either could not, or would not, do anything else, not for fame, or money, or any fortune that might come his way.

"Oh," Sangster exclaimed, "light, bring light."

Adam stirred, letting his arms drop to his sides.

"That is not for exhibition, or for public viewing, that is private."

Sangster looked at the painting, the dim light adding mystery to a face of unusual beauty, dark but softly so, its expression tender and sad, the eyes sending out a message of love but also bewilderment. Innocent and yet wordly, a paradox, he could not understand but longed to go forth and meet.

"Who?" he asked, "the love of your life?"

"My mother."

Gently, knowing the frail sensitivity of the artist he placed the picture back where he found it.

"I would like to take them all, Adam. I may call you Adam?"

Adam nodded. "I would like to hold an exhibition of your work," and then because there was no reaction, "an exhibition to be held in London.

"I have never sought fame. An exhibition in London means nothing to me."

"I cannot see how you can say such a thing. It has to mean something, it's the dream of hundreds of aspiring artists. Come now, you sell your work . . ."

"No. I take commissions, this work I did because I wanted to do. I haven't any noble ideas about starving for my art. I earn my own money and live my own life. Painting is the only way I know how to earn a living pleasurably."

Sangster could not see deeply into the man; there was so much beyond his words that a stranger could not grasp. He was deep with layers of pain, guarding his secrets too well. But Sangster was not a fool and was used to having his own way. He had guessed something of the artist's inner self, a small but not unimportant fact and he was not averse to using any method to gain his own ends, and so played his last card with a casualness that belied the cunning behind it.

"Surely your mother would be proud to see her son's paintings exhibited in the capital. It is a mother's nature to bask in the glory of her offspring."

Adam stared at him for a moment, almost angrily and then he smiled—when he smiled, Sangster thought, it was like the sun coming out after the storm.

"I suppose she would like it," Adam said.

The trap had been sprung and the bait taken.

Maureen was waiting by the large gnarled oak that was their regular meeting place. She was wearing a most becoming apple green day dress with a tight waist line that emphasized the ripening fullness of her body. Her bonnet was of matching shade and she carried a parasol on her shoulder of brown silk with a green fringe. She was turning it around and around in agitation and as he neared her and she saw him, he saw the tears spring angrily into her large gentle eyes. Her eyes were fathomless when he gazed into those dark depths he wanted to drown in their beauty.

"Oh Charles, I thought you were not coming," she said angrily. "I have waited so long and have felt like a woman of the town. People were looking at me."

"I am so sorry, but my aunt arrived unexpectedly and I was hard put to get away."

She was genuinely crying and it tore at his heart. He did not know what to do, how to comfort her, felt at once clumsy and irresponsible. They went around the oak tree and took their usual seat so that they would not be observed by any passers-by.

Once here he took her hand, holding it in his own, and then, since this did not appear to appease her, he unbuttoned her white glove, removed it so he might kiss and caress it free from covering.

He looked up, her cheeks were wetly crimson with her tears, the tears that seemed to spill in an endless flow from her eyes.

"Oh Maureen, what can I do? What can I say? I would not hurt you for the world, you know that."

He lent over and kissed her cheek, first one and then the other, drinking the very tears from her skin. She tasted of salt and of sweet apples; boldly he kissed the sides of her lips and then as she said nothing he put his mouth upon hers.

There was no objection, no rejection only compliance so that soon their arms were around each other and they kissed experimentally, finding it to their liking they lingered and lengthened until confused and frightened by the feelings that threatened to swamp them they broke tremblingly apart. She to touch her hair and adjust her bonnet and he to grip the bench and to stir the tiny pebbles in an ever-increasing circle with his foot.

"I love you," he said at last.

Maureen her heart galloping like a runaway horse did not speak. Charles lifted her hand and replaced her glove, fastening it with difficulty since his hands were trembling. He suggested they walk because if they continued to sit upon their secluded bench he would have to kiss her again.

People looked at them. It was not a guilty imagination,

this he realized with the side of him that was still rational. It was that Maureen was so very striking, being not only tall for a woman but well-shaped and good-looking with it. They made an exceptionally handsome couple, who would cause heads to turn. That they had managed to meet for so long without the Ayesthorpes' discovering the liaison could only be put down to luck.

"Maureen," Charles said, realizing that if they continued in the way they were doing there would only be greater trouble for them. "My parents have learned of our meetings."

"Oh," she groaned, pausing in her walk to look up at him, "and they are angry."

"No, not angry, but they have asked me not to meet you again."

She was momentarily furious, after all as the daughter of Josiah Ayesthorpe she was a person of some importance in her own right, and was considered eminently marriageable by a number of families in the town. But these families were merchants and manufacturers and not gentry, as were the Greys. Business people would not object to mother because their own near relations were suspect. However the Greys were an entirely different matter, they would not want Mama in their family, or tainting the blood of any forthcoming generations. In the wake of such reasoning she could only have her anger dampened by genuine despair. Oh, why oh why, had her father made such a bad marriage. He should have paid her off, given her money, anything rather than marry her. She was beginning to look on Mama as not her mother in her anguish she could not see that had Josiah not married Sarah she would not now be walking upon the Green with Charles Grey.

"Your father would doubtless issue a similar instruction to you."

Maureen did not know for certain that he would, there was hard feeling between the families but she might yet be able to persuade Papa to take a different view of the matter, after all he was exceptionally fond of his daughter; there was rapport between them such as never existed between Josiah and his son.

"I shall have to go and see him," Charles stated, taking Maureen by complete surprise.'

"Go and see Papa? Why should you go and see Papa?"

Charles oblivious to watchful eyes took Maureen's hands between his own holding them to his breast and looking down into her bemused eyes.

"We cannot go on meeting as we are doing; that is obvious. I must call upon him and tell him my intentions."

"*Your intentions*?"

"To marry you. You do want to marry me don't you, Maureen?"

Weakly she leaned against him, afraid less she had misheard him; she had dreamed of them marrying yet had never allowed it to become more than a dream, afraid to look upon it as an eventuality.

"But your parents . . ." she stammered.

"They will have to learn to accept it. If they cannot do so, then so be it. I want to share my life with *you*, Maureen and no other!"

Four

If worries were piles of paper, Josiah was certain that they would now be up to his chin. Trouble was seeping up from the factory floor, and there was his worry over his wife's health. Business and private life both in turmoil, no quiet sylvan spot where he could lay his head without feeling fearful of one or the other.

Young George entered the room, quietly and with an old sort of dignity which was odd considering his parents. The lad was a good sort and he had a natural flair for business that seemed to be all Ayesthorpe, but George Littlemoss for all that, was not his own son, and even though he was Lucy's child still it irked him to have to admit that perhaps one day the firm of Ayesthorpe would have, out of necessity, to become Littlemoss's.

"Uncle Joss, there's someone to see you."

"There's *always* someone to see me."

"It's Charles Grey."

His uncle stared mutely for a moment and then realizing just who Charles Grey was, and indeed what he represented he crudely told George what he should tell Charles Grey to do. His nephew was surprised because he had never associated his uncle with rough language. It did not at all go with his personality which, to the young George whose own father had an exuberant personality, was grave and serious.

"Oh damn," Joss said, "send him in," reading his nephew's dilemma.

The boy was quite like his father and his aunt, but even Josiah blinded as he was by prejudice, had to admit that

Charles Grey had a touch of sensitivity in his features that was not apparent in either Arabella or William.

"Well?" Josiah said, standing rather than offer his visitor a chair. "You look like a Grey," he said.

"Sir, I know there has been bad feeling between our families for many years."

"And do you know the reason?" Josiah asked, reaching for a cigar, taking it up and after biting off the end putting it between his teeth. He had the cigar lighted before the boy had stammered out what he had heard. That indeed he understood his father had once unintentionally insulted Mrs Ayesthorpe. Josiah laughed, an empty hollow macabre sound that went a long way to chilling the boy's blood and making him more nervous than ever.

"How gallant I am, to carry such a minor occurrence on through the years."

Charles could say nought to that. He did think it somewhat excessive but would not comment or state an opinion one way or the other, he dare not risk a refusal brought about by nothing more than an argument.

"Well what do you want?" Josiah asked bluntly. He was reminded of his father in the way he asked the question. Heaven forbid that he would ever become so blunt and so careless of people's feelings.

"I . . . I . . . I would like to marry your daughter sir."

"You would like to marry my daughter?" Josiah said reasonably. "To mend the breach between our families, I suppose. How noble."

"No sir . . . I . . . that is Maureen and I are in love and . . ."

"*Maureen and you are in love*! By what right do you call her Maureen? What are you talking about?"

Charles stammered and blushed and gasped and tried to explain, but Josiah would not let him finish the whole

68

story, interrupting each statement with a question that made the telling of it all from beginning to end an impossibility.

He had never in all his young life seen a man so angry, witnessed such a display of lack of control. He had thought for one moment that Josiah Ayesthorpe was going to strike him, his rage was terrifying. Much later Charles wondered that he had been able to leave the office with his life, let alone without a beating. However before he finally lost complete control of himself Mr Ayesthorpe himself left his office, striding out and slamming the door shut behind him, leaving Charles to wearily sink into the nearest chair.

Later the door opened and George Littlemoss came in and quietly and without ceremony poured a large brandy for Charles from the decanter upon his uncle's elaborate sideboard.

"I think you need this," was all he said.

"I hope you realize what you are doing, that you have considered it all very carefully."

"I have," Rosie murmured, her head upon his shoulder, his long lovely body wrapped within the silky folds of her newly washed hair.

"Your position will not be as secure as it was with whatshisname? I mean he is not much but he is of steady character."

"So is Mr Clegg, really he is and he will put me in a nice house in a new area. I have to think of my daughter. It is no good living here in the dwellings," she sat up, taking the warmth of her hair with her so that he drew the woollen blanket closer around him.

"If you are sure," Adam said.

"There is nothing else for me," and then looking over her shoulder at him. "*Is there*?"

69

He was quiet for a long time so that she felt her heart begin to beat faster, her pleasure decreasing in the wake of his long sad sigh.

"I am sorry, Rosie, I like you very much. You're kind and generous and I enjoy . . ."

"My body I know—you've told me before."

"It isn't just that!"

She could not be bitter or angry with him. Adam was the most totally honest person she had ever met. He never lied, or pretended feelings he did not have. She remembered the first day that she had met him, the day he moved in, noisily running up and down stairs, fetching his meagre belongings. She had asked him if he were a real artist and he had laughed, a laugh that had rid his face of anger and sadness.

Then she began to call on him, just to sit and chat in the evenings after her child was asleep, and on the nights when the man who kept her, was not visiting. He would make them tea and sometimes they shared a jug of black beer, warmed by the hot poker being plunged into the liquid when the nights were cold.

"You know," he said, one night looking directly at her and causing cold shivers to travel the length of her body, arousing in her feelings she had thought long dead, perished as they had on the battlefield of life. As a widow with a child she had been easy prey for the unscrupulous, but she had been sensible enough to find one protector, not for her a cold street corner or a house where a good half of her earnings would be paid to the madam. However Adam, the son of a gentleman and himself a gentleman had proved that she was not dead inside, not a machine of pleasure whose mind was a blank.

"I'd love to paint you, you really are a lovely young woman."

He made lots of sketches. Rosie as a working woman,

70

Rosie as a centurions wife, Rosie as a barmaid. Then one night when he had drank a goodly quantity of claret (given to him by his cousin George on one of his not infrequent visits). "Rosie don't be offended but would you let me paint you without your clothes?"

Rosie had flushed; Rosie Meadows after all these years of trying to make ends meet the only way she knew how was actually blushing because of something a man had said. He had been so upset, so apologetic earnestly swearing that there was nothing meant by it.

She went to him silently, turning her back, revealing to him the many hooks and eyes that held her dress together.

"I cannot manage myself," she said.

Nervously with fingers that trembled he undid the tiny fastenings, then watched as she quietly stepped out of the dress. Beneath she wore a chemise of thinnest cotton that was a little small for her. She swallowed, and he smiled.

"I did not ask in order that I should harm you. I spoke only as an artist."

"I know."

"Unpin your hair, then sit here . . ."

And paint her he did, never once looking at her with anything but an antiseptic eye so that she was utterly convinced that she was not attractive to him, that perhaps he did not even like women. She was frustrated by his indifference finding it increasingly difficult to be nice to her keeper, her thoughts obsessed only by Adam Ayesthorpe, and her need to have him.

Irritation, anger, all flooded through her as she lay still and supposedly relaxed while he silently dipped brush into palette and put paint upon canvas. It was too much, she felt like a piece of meat on a butcher's slab.

Surprising him she pulled herself from the position he

had instructed her to lie in and went to pull on her blue robe.

"Rosie?" he asked. "What's the matter?"

"You! You're the matter, you're not a man you're a painting machine with just as much feeling as those owd looms at your da's factory."

"Eh?"

"Well I'm a woman and I just cannot stand your indifference any longer."

"Oh Rosie," wearily he put down his brush and palette, wiping his hands upon a rag. "Rosie I have nothing to offer a woman."

"That does not surprise me!"

She went to leave, going to wrench open the door but he was there before her, his hand covering hers upon the latch.

"I do see you, love, believe me I do, in all your beauty. If I let myself think too much I could easily lose my self-control. I just happen to like you too much to offer you physical love, because that's all it could ever be with me. I don't have anything else inside me but a man's need."

She turned, pressing her back against the door.

"That is all I can accept. Oh, Adam, do you not see that is all either of us can give each other."

That night seemed aeons ago; now she would be leaving him, would not see him anymore, since Mr Clegg a wealthy merchant had promised to keep her in fine fashion, but in return had sternly demanded absolute faithfulness and because of her dependant child she knew she dared not risk seeing Adam ever again.

"I only have enough to keep myself," Adam continued, "I couldn't keep us both, or rather the three of us."

Not even if you wanted to! Her heart snapped angrily,

72

but to him she said nothing, it would be unfair and when she left him they would leave amiability between them that would make of their affair a pleasant memory.

Turning she returned to him, lying beside him and seeking his warm mouth with her own. Their passions met and overflowed and she knew it was going to be for the very last time.

The next day Adam took the London flyer, going on to greater things, they were both going on to greater things, to new lives. She as mistress to Mr Clegg and Adam to the real world of art, though she had to be cheered knowing that the painting he had done of her would be prominent in the exhibition, she only hoped Mr Clegg (who she was sure was something of a latent Methodist) never saw it.

Sangster greeted Adam enthusiastically, showing him around the gallery that would be a two weeks home for his paintings and from where he and his art would be launched into a well-primed art world.

"You are going to be famous Adam," Sangster assured him," and popular for that elusive personality, lots of ladies will want you to grace their salons."

The strange young man made no comment so that Sangster was unsure whether he was pleased, overawed or plain bored, and Sangster being Sangster liked the young provincial all the more. Intrigue, he thought, how they would love his air of intrigue!

When he viewed his paintings hanging in the gallery the night before the exhibition was due to open, he felt a rush of feeling erupt inside him. He thought of many things, and of one person in particular, and it was this thought that caused him to smile.

Sangster observing, asked why Adam smiled; it was rare that smile, genuine but rare, he should do it more often, Sangster thought.

"I was thinking of my grandfather, and what he would have said—something like—this is all right but is there any brass in it?"

"Ah," Sangster said, "and your mother what did she say?"

"I have no idea. I haven't seen her. I wrote her a letter and gave it to a friend to give to her."

"I imagined she would have been the first person you told," Sangster remarked somewhat perplexed. Adam said nothing and Sangster was loath to pry further.

"Grandfather would have told me to get a proper job. He wouldn't have approved at all. There was something very puritan in his make-up, the nobility of hard work, painting and writing would not be considered work in his book, and yet he could be kind too."

Sangster was silent. It was the longest speech his *protégé* had made about himself.

"He was kind to my mother once. Then she fell from favour, once you lost grandfather's affection you *never* regained it, no matter how hard you might try. Stubborn, autocratic, kind and yet unkind, a strange man, but fascinating."

"And your father, how did he get on with . . ? "

"I have no idea. Rosie is lovely, isn't she? I suppose if she was wealthy, poets would sing her charms, wealthy men would beat a path to her door and kings would leave their thrones for her. As it is she has to become the mistress of a narrow-minded hypocritical old bastard."

He does not like his father, Sangster gathered, paying no attention whatsoever to Adam's discourse upon the wretched Rosie.

Josiah raged, he did not see anything or feel anything other than anger. That his daughter had behaved so

74

irresponsibly, had been so wantonly careless of family and reputation as to have been meeting a man alone and unchaperoned.

"What sort of mother are you, madam?"

"Obviously one who has failed," she said, quietly from her position in the large armchair.

"*Failed, failed*? I'll say you have failed. Your son lives in an attic, and your daughter—*your daughter*—parades herself around town like the whore of Babylon, or is that the reason for her behaviour, the fact that she is your daughter?"

His wife pulled herself from out of her chair and went quietly and silently to stand by the bookcase, her back to him. In the interim he had gone to the door of the study and called loudly for their daughter.

"And I wonder how far she has gone in this little escapade, or is she so like you that she has to give herself to the first man that comes along."

Maureen came into the room, pale and tearful, trembling in fear of her father's wrath, for whatever else he had been in the past she had never seen him like this, so furious, so angry.

"I have been hearing things about you that I do not like, I have heard of meetings between you and one of the Greys that have culminated in his asking for your hand, well, what have you to say?"

"We're in love, Papa," she mumbled.

"In love? You're sixteen years of age and in love, well let me tell you, at sixteen you don't even know what love is. Has he any reason for wishing to marry you?"

"Papa?"

The question was so innocent, her eyes so wide and mystified he realised she had not been totally indiscreet. He let that side of the matter go but faced her sternly, trying to dampen his anger.

"You will not leave this house again without your mother or some other chaperone, you will not go to any parties without your mother or myself. You will not see Charles Grey again."

"Oh Papa, you don't understand, Charles wishes to marry me . . . "

"No daughter, or any of my family makes a marriage with the Grey family, besides his own family would *never* give their consent."

"It does not matter, Charles said . . . "

"I do not care about Charles or what he said. Even should the Greys approve I would not have it, I mean it, Maureen. There's plenty of time for you to find a suitable husband."

"The Greys would approve if it wasn't for m na. They would! They would! and there'd be no trouble but for her!"

Because her mother had not turned around, Maureen had felt suddenly very bold in her anguish and this together with hysteria and disappointment made her speak without consideration.

Papa went to his daughter and taking her in his arms soothed the sobs that erupted after her outburst, then he gently led her from the room.

Ann was by the dining-room door, she had the little kitchen servant by her side and he saw without registering it the child was shaking uncontrollably.

His anger subsided to become irritation, he led his daughter back to her room, then seeing her fall weakly upon her bed he left quietly. Meeting Letitia upon the stairs he told her to go and sit with Maureen and to see that she was not left alone.

There was nothing for it, he had to see the business over. His most unpleasant task lay before him. He had to go to the Greys for without their co-operation who knew what may occur.

Sarah heard the front door slam. She had not moved from her position by the bookcase. Tears spilled in an continuous stream, down her cheeks and onto the front of her dress.

Straightening she turned but must have jerked around too quickly for the room began to spin before her eyes. Weakly she leaned back against the wooden frame, imploring God to stop the sickening movements of the room. She took deep breaths and would have closed her eyes had she not been afraid of falling into the pit of oblivion. At last the room stilled and she was able to reach the chair and sink wearily into it. In her hand she held the letter that had come that day. Through tear-filled eyes she looked at it again. It was from her son telling her of his good fortune in being discovered by an art dealer and of the exhibition that was going to be held of his work in London. "You must come Mama, you must!" he had written.

She began to sob. He would imagine she had not gone because she did not care and she out of loyalty would be unable to tell him the real reason.

Ann came into the room, bustling and tutting and muttering mutinous sounds.

"Shall we put you to bed eh? Shall you lie still with a warm drink?" she asked tenderly.

Miserably Sarah screwed up the letter into a tiny ball and threw it into the fireplace.

"Yes Ann, put me to bed, that's obviously the best place for me."

Maureen left her bed afterwards and asked Letitia to bring her tea. She had to think about her problem calmly and see what had to be done.

It was Ann who brought the tea. Ann who used to nurse her and coddle her when she had been a child.

Maureen felt the tears begin again, she would tell Ann all about it and Ann would offer comfort and advice.

Ann put the tea-tray down upon the small table and before Maureen could ask her to sit awhile Ann crossed the room, raised her hand and slapped Maureen soundly across the cheek.

Maureen leapt to her feet, her hand across her stinging cheek, feeling anger begin to take the place of amazement.

"How dare you strike me!"

"How dare I strike you? I'll say how I dare. You're not too big for a tanning though you may think yourself so, well I'll tell you summat for nowt, I don't think much of you, for all your airs and your graces and your, I'll take tea now if you please. I don't care about your romances or your gentlemen friends because I think you're a poor do! Your mother—yes stick your nose in the air—came from nowt, we all know that, when she were your age she'd a baby to attend to an' a husband who'd have frozen Russia in the middle of winter, but I'll tell you *Miss* Ayesthorpe that your mother always was and always will be a lady because being a lady 'as nowt to do with where you came from. It 'as to do with what's inside you, and lastly I'll tell you this, you're not going to make it. You, like your grandmother before you, will never be a lady, not till all of hell freezes over."

"You're fired," Maureen cried.

Ann said nothing, nor did she smile or remonstrate, or tell Miss Maureen Ayesthorpe that hiring and firing was none of her business. She left the room as quickly as she had come . . .

The family were in the salon enjoying a pre-dinner drink and if Mr Ayesthorpe would wait the flunkey complete with powdered wig and silk pants, would see if Sir

William was free.

It was twenty years or more since Josiah had stepped into this elegant house. Years ago he had been quite at home amongst its luxurious appointments, now he felt only a sense of great unease.

It was not beyond the realms of possibility that Grey would have his flunkeys throw him, not only out of the house, but off his property and Josiah knew that if that did happen much more trouble would ensue, knew it by the feeling of bad temper that still lingered inside him.

It had taken much courage to come here to face Grey and to actually speak to him after all these years, but he felt the visit justified. Sir William would have to control his son as he, Josiah, was controlling his daughter.

The doors to the salon opened, with nervous apprehension Josiah took a deep breath.

"Josiah, how lovely to see you! Just like old times."

Arabella! It was Arabella floating towards him in a creation of white lace that made her appear like a beautiful fairy queen; the in-drawn breath caught in his windpipe and made him cough.

"Arabella," he managed at last.

"Do come through, my brother and his wife are within. I am so pleased you came. This feud is so childish, feuds are for the wild clansmen of Scotland not for civilized English folk. Come . . . "

She took his arm leading him forward so that he was drowning in lace and exotic scent. He was at once thrown into confusion. Never had he imagined that of all people Arabella would be at Grey Manor, nor after their last meeting that she would greet him so effusively.

Sir William was by the fireplace. His wife whom Josiah did not know sitting upon a settee close by.

"My dear Ayesthorpe," Sir William said, extending his hand and coming forward. "How nice to see you."

79

More than bewildered Josiah accepted the clasp. "Come and meet the wife, Elizabeth this is Joss Ayesthorpe my old-time friend and companion in many a scrape is that not so, Joss?"

Lady Elizabeth with a slight smile extended her pale hand to Josiah, registering and relishing his confusion, and confused he was for he had expected many things but affability was not one of them.

"Have a drink, glass of claret, or would you prefer spirits?" Sir William asked.

"Er no, claret would be fine."

"I know why you're here, Joss, I fully expected I should have to do the calling. Dash nuisance isn't it, the children imagining they are in love."

"Oh but so romantic," Arabella whispered, "the Ayesthorpes and the Greys, they seem inexplicably drawn to each other."

Josiah turned to look at her, there was a wistfulness about her that touched him, he remembered the old days, days spent here or those at the Greys' villa in Florence. In his utter confusion he began to see them as glorious balmy times, forgetting the hurt inflicted upon him by Arabella.

"Please sit down, Mr Ayesthorpe," Lady Elizabeth murmured, indicating a place beside her. "I think we have a solution to the problem. I take it you do not wish your daughter to marry Charles?"

"I . . . no, no of course not. She is much too young."

"Good, good. Well then we have decided to send Charles abroad I think that best under the circumstances, don't you?"

Josiah thankfully agreed. With Charles Grey out of the way there would be no temptation for Maureen to disobey him. He would now have her chaperoned at all times. If she did have her mother's nature it would be not only practical but necessary.

"Now that is solved perhaps we can entreat you to dine with us," Sir William said.

His head spun, the food, the elegant dining-room, the low intimate candlelight, the champagne and oysters and saddle of lamb, all succulently prepared, his head was turned momentarily. Here with these aristocratic landowners he could forget his troubles, shelve the problems of his factory and the workers.

Grey and his family were not interested in discussing trade or the state of things, they talked about music and the theatre. Hunting and riding and country pursuits. Given the circumstances he could not remember enjoying an evening more.

It was late when he arrived home. Ernest had been instructed to wait up for him and was waiting to finally lock the door for the night. After bidding him goodnight Josiah went into his dressing-room. He looked at his reflection in the glass, saw himself as still quite young, a man indeed in the prime of life. Quietly he undressed, leaving his clothes over a chair, an unusual thing for him to do; he was a tidy man who liked things neat and orderly. After slipping into a robe and raking a hand through his blond hair he went into the bedroom.

There was a faint light upon his night table. His wife was already in bed, her hair loosely spilling across the pillows.

She heard him come in and opened her eyes.

"I am not asleep," she said softly.

There was no reply. After removing his robe he joined her in the bed, turning onto his side and after extinguishing the light lying down.

"Things were amicable then?" she asked. She could smell brandy and cigars and scent. Expensive scent. Her heart was a hard knot inside her, the pain unbearable.

"Are you not speaking to me?" she asked.

She sighed and then lay still. There was a bright moon that inched its way through a chink in the curtains, she watched moonlight spread over the cornices until they became misty and blurred, drowned by a sea of tears.

The following day as he arrived at his factory he was confronted by an angry mob. His workers to whom he had tried to be loyal had decided to strike, their agitators a group of men led by Joe Marsden, a man whose own sister worked in his home!

Once he had managed to gain access into the factory he saw that not all the workers had indeed joined the strike, but those who had not were too small a group to make production a feasible proposition. Besides he feared what the mob would do to those who had decided to stand by their master.

"Right," Josiah said to George who stood nearby quite calmly. "Lock up, give these fellows a weeks wages for their loyalty, see them on their way then we go home. I'll not be dictated to by a mob, no matter how right they think their action."

Josiah eventually arrived home. As he and George left the factory the angry crowd had pressed around them, there had been a moment when he was certain they intended harm, that they would pull him down onto the ground and kick him to death, it was there on the air, violence. Although he wanted to panic, wanted to push and shove and free himself he did not do so, merely stood still meeting them eye to eye, his face expressionless so that eventually the men broke ranks and he and George were able to walk on.

"My God," George muttered, "I thought we'd had it." His uncle smiled reassuringly and at the same time was filled with admiration for his nephew who too had not panicked but had taken his lead from him.

Now at home he wanted to think about the best method of dealing with the situation. There were three alternatives open to him, all he had to do was decide which to take. Whether to take on Irish labour which was plentiful and cheap, or to bring weavers from the outlying districts, men so clemmed they would be happy to work for any price, or to keep the factory locked. The latter would cause him to lose an order, financially he could afford to do this but at what damage to his reputation?

His home was silent. Sarah was nowhere downstairs. He found his daughter in her room sitting with Letitia, she looked up at him expectantly and then seeing that he had not changed his mind she turned sulkily away.

Sarah was not in their room either; he went downstairs once more and when he reached the study he rang for Ann.

"Do you know where my wife is?"

"Aye," the woman answered, with unconcealed impudence.

"Well?" he snapped, "where?"

"She's gone away," Ann said.

"Away, away, what do you mean away?"

"Away. Left. Whether for a short break or permanently I can't say."

He slammed his palm down on the desk. Damn these insufferable women.

"Where has she gone? When did she leave? What is she about? I told her she must look to her daughter!"

"Her daughter can look to herself," Ann said, "as she had to when she were her age. She's left you, like she left you before only this time she might not come back. Might not *have* to come back since there's someone as can look after her proper."

"Damn you, Ann, what are you talking about?"

"I'm talking about you. Yes *you*! What you said to her last night, what everyone heard you say about her, and what are you I ask myself, to set yourself up as anyone's judge."

"Shut up," Josiah said, "Shut up or get out!"

"Oh I shall go, I don't want to serve you. I never did ever want to serve you. Even when you were little you were full of your own importance. Well to me you're nowt Joss Ayesthorpe, never was and never 'as been. You've always blamed her for everything, well let me tell you summat what everyone knows. She never forced you into anything, never asked nor probably ever wanted. She gave you a gift once and you've never ceased to throw it back in her face."

Josiah stared at her, at this woman, his servant like his workers turning savagely against him, like his son had done before them, but before he could speak or protest or move she had left the room slamming the door shut behind her.

Wearily he sank into his chair putting his hands up to his throbbing temples. He could not understand what had happened.

There were many people at the gallery, Sangster from a vantage point kept his eye upon the main entrance as much as he possibly could, and he happened to be looking in the direction when a woman, alone, made a tentative entrance, pausing and looking and waiting almost expectantly.

There was a familiarity about her, so he had the vaguest of feelings that he knew her, and then he realized that he did not know her at all, but was aware instantly who she was.

Wordlessly he nudged Adam and nodded towards the

84

door, when he looked in the direction and saw who had arrived a smile erupted over his features and then he was gone, pushing his way and running where the way was clear.

"Mama!" he exclaimed, reaching her at last and gathering her up in his arms. "You came! You came!"

His joy at seeing her was such that it made her at long last realize that her rebellion was worthwhile and indeed that it was right.

"Adam, I'm so proud of you," she exclaimed, brushing away tears that would not be controlled.

"Sangster said that. He said you would be proud of me. Are you here alone?" he asked quickly, looking beyond her for another figure.

"Yes, quite alone."

"Where are you staying?"

"With the Sisters of Charity."

"The Sisters of Charity!" he exclaimed and then laughed, "That's all prayer and porridge. You must come and stay with me. I have large apartments."

"Oh Adam, it isn't all prayer and porridge, it's very nice."

"Nevertheless you will stay with me. Oh, Mama, Mama!"

She took his hand and held it tightly.

"You must show me around, I must see everything."

With adoring eyes he gazed at her. She was wearing a silk gown of a deep lemon shade, with a hat that had a feather that curled around her cheek. The lemon became her, flattering her darkness and the curling feather gave her a flirtatious, piquant look.

"I'm pleased to see that you have discarded the mourning."

"Yes, a little too soon, but I have decided to be unconventional, besides I'm sure your grandfather would not mind. Get out o' those weeds, Sarah, he'd say, you look like an old crow."

Adam laughed, tucking her arm in his and going to lead her around the exhibition. Everyone else could go hang, he thought, he wanted only to hear what Mama thought. No one else mattered.

"And Papa," he asked, "what did he say when you told him you wanted to come to London to see me?"

"He did not say anything," she said quietly.

"I find that hard to believe!"

"He said nothing to me," Sarah gently insisted," and please let's not talk about Papa. Please!"

"All right, now you must look and tell me the whole truth."

Mama looked and admired just as everyone else had done, although other people's admiration was nothing to him, praise from Mama was as nectar to the gods, he drank deep and long and quizzed her upon every point she made, extracting every morsel of praise from her.

"Rosie is very beautiful," she said.

"How do you know she's Rosie?"

"*I know*," she looked up at him archly, "she is nicer than I thought. Oh!' she exclaimed going on, "that's the little Connolly boy from my school, surely it is he?"

"Yes."

"How marvellous, you've captured his mischief and his piety. He's an angel of a child. Did you know that Anthony is going to buy him an apprenticeship?"

"Ah, Anthony, your partner in crime," he teased.

"My partner in crime?"

"The crime," he said in a fair imitation of Grandfather Ayesthorpe," of educating the poor when you should be sending them as fodder for t'mill."

She laughed, a tinkling delightful sound.

"Oh darling," she squeezed his arm. "I'm so happy for you, so very, very, happy."

"I in't so sure this courtin' and then marryin' is such a good thing."

"Whyever not, *fach*, don't I turn my money over to you for you to put in the little black box, then don't I stay away from the gin shops, is it? And aren't I nice-looking?"

"Your blooming head's liable to fall off, seeing as its too flipping big for your body!"

"Oh darling of mine, don't be such a sour old faggot and give us a kiss."

"Love don't last, kisses don't last, it's all babies and scrapping from what I can see."

It was cold today and she had her shawl wrapped tightly around her head and shoulders but the teasing wind brought tendrils of hair to dance impishly about her small face.

He had met her after after his work and they had had tea at his lodgings. It was always the same when she had been to her brothers. Joe and Ellie's state never failed to make her depressed.

Her brother had also forbidden her to keep company with Dick Jones, not only that but he had told her in no uncertain terms that he would not give his consent to their marriage. Jane was too kind-natured to see that it was fear of losing the money she so generously gave them that caused his attitude, but Dick saw it all very clearly, and was determined that Joe, by hook or crook, would not get his own way.

Because of the lock out, or strike at the Ayesthorpes', Jane's was the only wage Joe and Ellie had. If Joe had been anyway reasonable Dick too would have tipped him the odd copper or two because he had in him a sense of family, but he would be damned if he would help the man when he was obviously being spiteful and selfish.

Dick was walking her back to the Ayesthorpes at Newton now, and they would not be able to meet again until Sunday. He loved her, this tiny creature with her hard way of speaking. She was tough but tender, the sort of woman who would work with him and save with him. He was uncertain what he wanted but he knew it to be more than he had.

They passed a gap in the hedge that Jane pretended not to have seen, but he laughed and pulled her through it, then away from any passers-by took her in his arms and kissed her tenderly.

"Am sorry Dickie, I know I've been grumbling but I'm so sad what with Missies gone and everything."

"She's not back yet?" Dick asked, pulling her closer to him. He did not know Jane's mistress but he knew it was she who, when Jane had told her of her courtship, had given Jane the tiny black chest for her savings, and she who had been teaching Jane practical sewing.

"No and no one knows for sure where she's at, but Ann I think knows but she 'as gone, staying with her sister over Collyhurst way, an' that Letitia so fancy like as she thinks she's housekeeper now, and the Master so angry all the time and Miss Maureen a weepin' and wailin' 'cos her lover 'as been sent to France and places on from there. It's horrible."

"Never mind, *fach*, if we save as hard as we can perhaps we can find a little house to rent, I am looking all the time . . ."

"But Joe won't sign for us to marry, I just told you so."

"Don't worry about that," Dick said with such firm assurance that she felt certain that things would be bound to turn up all right.

He kissed her again, longingly, lingeringly, his embrace closer. "Come, come lay upon the grass for a moment . . . " his voice was thick and pleading, tempting so she hesitated a moment or two, and he thought that this time he had won, but no she broke from him, pulling her shawl over her head once more and saying she must be off. It was always the same, she would allow him no more than kisses and holding, resolutely refusing even to let him touch or caress her. She was well brought up, he reasoned walking home to Ancoats, and he would not like it anyway were she to be free with him, but oh if only she would give a little more.

When he reached Ancoats the main street was alive with revellers coming and going from the gin shops and beer houses. In his pocket he had a sixpence so he went into the beer house for a mug of ale. It was dark and grim inside and hardly a pleasant sort of place, but it did give him an idea.

Life indeed at the Ayesthorpe's was quite grim. Jane seemed to have lost her incentive for polishing everything until it gleamed when there was no mistress to admire and praise and encourage. Miss Maureen stayed mostly in her own room and Mr Ayesthorpe spent his days and most of the evening in his study. He was concerned about the strike much more, the servants said, than he was about his missing wife.

Letitia liked Mr Ayesthorpe, or as Jane thought to herself, fancied him, and said it was not right that she had taken herself off when he was so worried about his business amongst other things.

"She's done it before," Letitia told Jane, "left him. I would never leave him. A wife should always be loyal to her husband and obey his word."

Jane paid no attention. Letitia was a spinster who knew nowt. She might think Mr Ayesthorpe handsome and romantic but Jane knew better. He had shouted mean things to his wife, in so cruel a manner that it had reduced Jane to tears and if it did that to herself, who was only an observer, what had it done to her beloved mistress.

Mrs Ayesthorpe's associate trustee of the little school had come calling with a black-robed priest who Jane dared not look at lest he put a spell on her, and make off with her to the nearest nunnery, though she did not mind the other gentleman, he always gave her a piece of fruit, an apple or an orange depending upon what he had with him.

"Mrs Ayesthorpe isn't here, and their business is nothing to do with me," Mr Ayesthorpe had said after Jane had announced them.

"What shall I say then?"

"What shall I say then, *sir*!" he snapped. "Say that Mrs Ayesthorpe is away, and that is to apply to anyone else who calls on her."

The men passed a look between them, curious, surprised, so that for a moment Jane was tempted to tell the reasons Mrs Ayesthorpe was not available, but in the end she said nothing. After all Mr Ayesthorpe may tell her to leave for betraying the private business of the family, and she could not afford to lose a job that paid her a fair wage and which also gave her a roof over her head.

"Oh please come back," she prayed, "please, please Missies come back!"

Later the same day the Littlemoss's came to visit, mother and son. George, Jane liked, he was gentle, he always had a kind word, different from his mama who was an imperious woman.

On this occasion they did not give Jane time to announce their arrival, but strode without a word into Josiah's study, even Mr George seemed to have forgotten common courtesy in his haste, and Jane only hoped Mr Ayesthorpe was not going to blame her for their irregular behaviour.

Lucy was still in mourning for her father, but what mourning Josiah thought. Her dress was all frills, flounces and lace and with her large bonnet helped only to make her over-ripe body seem even larger. Poor Lucy, he thought, the years had stolen her beauty with cruel revenge. She ate too much, doing little exercise to compensate her appetite, but worse of all she called her mirror a liar, not believing the reflection that told of loose flesh and a too red complexion. The laudanum she took for her constant headaches aiding her in her deception. Though Josiah, along with Lucy's husband and two sons and countless friends, knew nothing of her addiction.

Josiah could have screamed at the sight of his sister. He did not need at this time in his life to hear her whines and complaints, having neither the patience or tolerance at that moment to call up sufficient dignity to put up with this visit, that he anyway saw only as an intrusion on his private life.

Lucy sat upon the chair that was placed before the desk, behind which Josiah sat, George stood at her side, stern and with an arm along the back of his mother's chair somewhat protectively.

"Is Sarah not about?" Lucy asked, turning her head this way and that, anything so it appeared than look directly at her brother.

"She's left, whether permanently or temporarily I cannot say."

"Left? She's left you *again*," Lucy exclaimed, as if her sister-in-law made a habit of leaving her husband. "Oh, I don't understand Sarah, I really do not. She is impossible!"

"It's her dark Celtic side," Josiah said moderately, "something from which we Anglo-Saxons don't suffer."

"What are you talking about, Joss?" Lucy snapped the question, glancing at her son whose frank gaze caused her to fidget.

"Mama has something to tell you, Uncle Joss," he said, "do you not, Mama?"

"Oh," Lucy squirmed and fluttered, Josiah felt his patience wearing down, feeling a need to be very rude to his guests.

"Come, Mama," George insisted.

"Well, you see, Josiah, I have been, I am very fond of Maureen. Not having a daughter of my own, and she is so like me, I mean when I was her age, so bright and lovely, but of course she is much too tall—I do hope she has stopped growing . . ."

"Mama," George cautioned, seeing his uncle's already white tense face becoming more so.

"Oh yes, yes, give me time. Well Sarah, you know how she does not like going out and about in society, I mean with people like the Greys, and Maureen is only young, she likes to dance, and to be seen about, just as I did at her age, Sarah can be so dull at times—not liking things like that, well Sarah let me act as Maureen's chaperone and—and well I knew about her and Charles Grey . . . they were so in love and . . ."

She started as Josiah brought his palm down on the desk.

"You mean you knew! You knew and you did not tell me. You knew my daughter was meeting that boy . . ."

"Yes," Lucy lisped.

"And," prompted George.

"I used to let them meet at our house sometimes. Oh, Josiah please do not look at me that way, I did not know they were meeting on the Green as well."

"I could murder you Lucy, willingly and wantonly."

Lucy jerked back as Josiah stood as though he would indeed carry out his threat, but no, he paced across the room thoughtfully and went to look out of the window.

At last he spoke, so low that Lucy arose from the chair and went to his side the better to hear him.

"I was dreadful to Sarah," he was saying, "I thought her careless of Maureen."

"Well she could have done more for the girl, that has to be said, but then Sarah could never see anyone else but that boy of hers, I suppose now she's gadding about London with him. I never could abide that child, though I never showed it."

Josiah turned and looked at her, not even hearing her, engrossed only by the worrying thought that he had sent Sarah away.

"Have you decided anything yet about the strike, Uncle Joss?" George asked cutting across his uncle's thoughts.

"Yes, we keep locked. They will come back on my terms and in my time. No one is going to dictate to me what I should and should not do. I pay my workers more than any other owner and by God they shall not get a penny more."

"I thought we might see one or two of the ringleaders and . . ."

"I do not hold meetings with a mob," his uncle snapped. It was not like his uncle to be so adamant, George came to realize that his stand had more to do with Aunt Sarah's departure than with the duplicity of his workers.

"I think we should leave Mama, Uncle Joss will wish to be alone."

"It's not right to leave you Joss, why don't you come home with us and we can sup together," so saying she tucked her arm around him as if to lead him away. "Arabella's in town did you know?"

"I . . . yes, yes I did. I saw her when I went to sort this business over Maureen and Grey out."

"She is still so very lovely, I wonder what her secret is?" Lucy mused.

Josiah looked at her for a moment and then, "I thank you for your invitation Lucy, but I cannot come home with you. I must stay here for when Sarah returns."

"She wants a good spanking!"

"I wonder where she had gone," he said.

"I told you, probably in London with Adam."

"With Adam in London. What do you mean? I didn't know Adam was in London."

They came along the street holding hands as if they were a young courting couple; and indeed they looked so perfect together that his heart ached jealously at the sight of them.

She was exceedingly gracious as if she had just come in from the garden and not missing this past week. He was surly and cool.

He had been standing in the street for one and a half hours and just for a moment he thought that his son was not going to invite him into his home.

Anyway in the event it was Sarah herself who said they should go in and have some tea.

She was so different, so assured and confident, happy even, utterly without remorse. It was hard for him to reconcile himself to her attitude, after all he had had— and still had—his back pressed against the wall by business worries, had been concerned about her, about her disappearance, her pregnancy and yet here she was, quite content in the society of her son.

Adam's new surroundings were in startling contrast to

those Josiah had last seen his son occupying. He now had the whole of the downstairs of an early Georgian house in a quiet tree-lined street of similar houses.

It was tastefully furnished but with much clutter. The apartment belonged to a gentleman who was travelling upon the Continent so that Adam had a three-months lease. Though he was uncertain whether or not he would remain in London. It was Sarah who ventured the information seeing to the tea things and chattering all the time like an excited little girl.

Josiah felt honour bound to comment upon his son's success, and the exhibition where he had gone on his arrival in London.

"I am overawed by your talent," he said, but softly, meeting Adam's gaze directly. His son was lounging elegantly against an oak dresser, to this statement he merely inclined his head.

Josiah felt suddenly angry at what he saw as his son's unreasonable attitude, not only was it unfair it was unjustified; he had done nothing whatsoever to deserve such contempt. He looked now at Sarah but she was looking down into her cup as if there lay her future.

"I have to talk to you, Sarah," Josiah said, pleadingly.

"Yes," was all she said.

Adam sighed, straightened, came over to the chair where his mother was sitting and leaning over pressed a tender kiss upon her cheek.

"I have to see Sangster," he said, "I'll see you later."

So saying he left the room. Josiah groaned slightly, putting a weary hand over his eyes.

"Do not say anything!" Sarah cautioned.

"I was not going to, I am well aware that as far as you are concerned his bad manners are an acceptable part of his personality," steadily she met his gaze. "I am sorry," he said, "but he is so obstinate towards me. I know you think that I do not have any feelings but I assure you I hurt as much as anyone else."

Sarah stood, went to him and standing in front of him put a comforting hand upon his shoulder.

"I love you, and I love him but Adam wants all my love. It's as simple as that."

Josiah put his hand over hers. "Why did you run away from me?"

"I did not run away, I decided I wanted to share my son's success. This was to be my very last fling, the one and only chance to kick up my heels."

"Surely not!"

"You forget I shall have a young baby to attend to shortly."

"Have you told Adam?"

"No, and nor shall I for the moment. However, I have had my fling now and I have had a glorious time and am ready to come home."

"What I said . . . how I was . . . I want to explain."

"No. It does not matter, you were not wrong in certain respects. I have neglected Maureen, I kept in the background to give her a better chance. I know what a lot of people say about me, however it has not worked, so I shall come out of hiding and she will have to learn to accept having a mother who is suspect. I cannot change it for her, no matter how hard I might wish to do so, and in other matters I am not prepared to compromise."

Five

Sarah went over her belongings, the tiny things like ornaments and miniatures that had been collected over the years, the various gifts and trinkets given to her by her husband, her son or friends and admirers. Some valuable, others not so, but each holding a special place in her heart.

Since coming home she had been flooded by contentment and ease, despite the tantrums of her daughter, within Sarah glowed.

This peace was not entirely due to the fact that she had seen how her husband needed her, but it had something to do with it.

She had successfully brought him to heel; though his remarks had hurt she knew she could have had a blistering row with him, and that she was well able to verbally wound him in return, but this time she had needed more, needed to test her independence, to see if her wings would still enable her to fly.

As a woman she had to rely upon Josiah for her livelihood. Her father was dependent upon her for his livelihood, therefore she had nowhere to turn should she wish to leave her husband and home, no doting parents able to open their doors while her husband, if he wished, could petition court in order to have her returned to him. However, now she had a truly independent son. Adam had no money of his own, yet he had struck out and carved out a successful future for himself. Every one of his paintings had been sold and already he had a handful of commissions to produce more, and what was of more importance was that her son would never close his doors to her. Not that she wished to use him as a convenience, but it was good at long last to know that there was an alternative for her.

She loved Josiah, but she had vowed a long time ago never to allow herself to be used as a doormat for him and made certain too that he always pursued her, and pursue her he had done!

She was not satisfied with her possessions and too was a little sick inside, sitting quietly in her sitting-room looking, without really seeing at a sulky Maureen embroidering cushion covers which were destined for Sarah's school. Sarah had set her daughter about the task which Maureen had begun because she sensed an iron-like hardness about her Mama which was different from her usual indolence.

Josiah wanted her again that night. She knew him so well, she could tell his every mood. All through dinner she sensed his impatience, the way he toyed with his food and how he did not listen attentively to his daughter's chatter.

I must not feel smug and over confident Sarah told herself, but it was so glorious a feeling that it was difficult to resist the temptation to bask in vanity, after all they had been married for over twenty years!

Later Maureen implored her father to play cards with her and Sarah gave her daughter support. Truthfully Sarah felt sorry for her daughter, it was obvious that her infatuation with Charles Grey went deep and her mother was not so old or so insensitive that she did not recall her own pain.

Josiah reluctantly gave in, giving his wife a damning look as she said she would retire early.

"Are you not well, Mama?" Maureen asked, feeling solicitous towards Mama because she had managed to persuade Papa to play her at cards.

Sarah looked at Josiah and then turned back to her daughter saying: "I am going to have a child."

"Oh!" Maureen gasped, looking from Mama to Papa, who looked away, then returned her gaze to Mama once more.

"I thought—oh," she stopped far too embarrassed to continue, and biting her lower lip to cover her distress.

"It is all right," Mama said, "I am quite well."

So saying she kissed her daughter's cheek, then after bidding her husband goodnight left the room.

She was not sleeping when he arrived but was reading. When he entered the room she put a bookmark at her page, closed the book and placed it upon her night table.

"I want to talk to you," she said softly.

"Well I most certainly do not want to *talk* to you!"

"Seriously," she said, smiling as he sighed, then he sat upon the edge of the bed and began to remove his neck cloth, giving her a nod to speak. "I have been going through all those possessions I have collected over the years, knick-knacks that are near my heart. Two silver snuff boxes, my two golden thimbles and a piece of china have gone."

"Gone? What do you mean gone?"

"They are not there. First there was my favourite vase which disappeared, now these items."

"Oh God! A thief in our midst on top of everything else. It must be that little Marsden chit . . ."

"No, I do not believe that Jane would steal from me. *I know it*—don't frown—I'm absolutely certain. That leaves Ann."

"Ann? I meant to ask you about that, why has she been reinstated?"

"Because I love her as I would love my own mother. So we know it cannot be Ann, it isn't Letitia, she may wish to steal you from me but not my trinkets."

"Steal me, what do you mean, steal me indeed?"

"Oh she has a soft spot for you."

"Really?" he took her hand holding it tightly. "So that leaves Ernest and Cook, both with us for ten years, it seems unlikely that it's either."

"Quite so. What do we do? I hate suspicion and accusation, do we mention it, or do I forget it?"

"You do not forget it. Those things are your own, given to you by people who love you. I am reluctant to call in the police though."

"Heaven's above, I'd never involve the police, but if it is not the servants then who else would take away my things?"

"I have no idea," Josiah said, "anyway, we will call everyone together and tell them, it's only fair and despite what you say I am all for putting the blame on Jane Marsden."

But Sarah was adamant, insisting that she knew people and Jane was neither a thief nor a liar and, furthermore stated that his prejudice against Jane had a lot to do with her brother being one of the strike leaders.

So chastened he went to his dressing-room to prepare for bed. When he returned Sarah was reading again, her black curling hair spread out over her body and down her back, long and thick and as luxurious as ever.

"And if all that chat was for the sole intent of putting my mind off love I have to tell you that you have failed."

She laughed gaily, threw the book to one side and stretched out a hand to clasp his arm and so to pull him towards her.

"It is simply a question of wanting the unattainable and of being bored by the attainable. I was the same as a child if you recall, never wanting my own toys but desperate to have those that belonged to others. If they relinquished their toys easily I broke them, if there was a struggle to take the toys I appreciated them for quite some time."

They rested their horses on a slight incline that looked over the lush Mersey Valley, where the river ran in a bold loop between green watermeadows. The sky was hard bright blue, here and beyond to the southern tip of the horizon. Beyond to the north it became dark as a great circle of black smoke smothered the sky and hung ominously over the town.

"But Joss Ayesthorpe is so . . ."

"Middle class, I know, but it's that about him that appeals. His narrowness, it sort of teases me, not only that, he is the most beautiful man I have ever seen, and that goes for past and present."

William laughed, admiring his sister, her delicate fair beauty enhanced by her masculine dark brown riding habit.

"Now is my time, I have done my duty to the family . . ."

"No," William said unable to resist the temptation to push her from the pedestal of self-importance. "You have failed in one respect, you have not had any heirs. My children will have no dukes to call cousin."

Arabella reddened, jerked her horse around and then cantered off back towards town. William laughed, he never could resist taking Arabella down by a peg or two, even though the thought of her attempted seduction of Joss Ayesthorpe delighted him. Anything to disturb the peaceful life that little Irish gypsy had carved out for herself.

Jane was weeping into her apron, unable to bring herself under control in spite of Ann's remonstrating with her. In the end Cook made her a cup of tea and even gener-

101

ously spiced it with a drop of her own rum.

"No one thinks it was you took her things, lass."

"T'int that," Jane wailed, "I know she don't think it was me, it's just the thought that someone 'as been stealing from her, and her as would give you owt you asked for if she could."

"Aye that is hard, those gold thimbles were given her by her fellow trustees after she'd been on the school board ten years. Sentimental value, that's what they all are, that's what makes me wonder . . ." Ann murmured, "sip your tea now Jinny and pull yourself together."

All the servants had been ordered to gather in the parlour; there had been a little apprehension but no real terror; the general consensus of opinion was that the family were going to move house, perhaps further into the country, or perhaps nearer to town, though this seemed unlikely, for the town had grown worse in recent years with smoke and smells so putrid that all those who could were moving to the very edges, leaving the interior to the working class, who had no opportunity to do likewise.

All then had received a shock when Mrs Ayesthorpe told them of her missing trinkets, even though she firmly stated her belief in their innocence. She asked each person, who had been visiting the house, perhaps while she was away, or had any outside workers been labouring at the house for any reason, chimneysweeps or men brought in to carry out any household repair—or—reluctantly she asked with darkening cheeks, perhaps some men from the mill had called to see Mr Ayesthorpe and he had been out, or not available. But there was no one, no one apart from Lucy and George, and a shivering Jane also informed her, Mr Harrop and a priest, but they had only stayed in the hallway. Besides it was unlikely that they would steal, or more especially take something they had given to her in the first place.

No matter how nicely Mrs Ayesthorpe explained or questioned, still it left the servants with a nasty taste in their mouths, each vowing that they themselves would discover the culprit. Letitia and Ernest glaring meaningfully at little Jane.

Ann though had other ideas and later that day when an opportunity presented itself she sought out her mistress.

Sarah was alone at the time, sitting upon the window seat looking out onto the rain-soaked gardens, wondering if the pounding rain would scatter the petals from the first summer roses.

The gardens abounded with roses, of every colour and size, roses were her favourite flower, she loved their shape, their smell and the velvety softness of their petals.

"I was thinking," Ann said, taking a seat beside her mistress. Sarah looked at her questioningly, remembering how kind she had been to her when she had been a child, the love and tenderness bestowed upon her as she had become a new and very unhappy bride, years of faithful devoted service and friendship so that she made a mental note with something akin to panic to entreat Josiah to make provisions for Ann in her old age, by way of a pension of some sort.

"You're not going to be cross with me if I say what I've been thinking."

"No," Sarah said, yet doubtfully, putting her hand upon her stomach.

"Well, love makes you do funny things, and I thought —well as he was away from you he might like to have something to remember you by. Something to fondle and to look at, a little piece that you have touched and looked at."

Sarah met Ann's gaze steadily.

"Adam? You mean you think Adam stole from me?"

"Not stole exactly, but borrowed."

"But he would ask! Surely he would say Mama give me something of yours for a keepsake, yes I am sure he would."

"He might have done it on the spur of the moment, that day he brought little Jinny to you, he was upset with having to come to the house, and was anxious to be off in case he met Master, maybe he just saw your things and acted desperately."

"No! No! Perhaps my thimbles or a snuffbox, but a china ornament and, and a vase, no I cannot see it, Ann."

Ann sighed. It was no use speaking further on the matter, to do so may annoy Sarah Ayesthorpe, nevertheless Ann was convinced that she had discovered the culprit; the boy was deeply enamoured of his mother, sentimentally attached to her, too much for his own good Ann was certain, but that was beside the point. It was the sort of thing he would do—dramatic and sadly romantic that was Adam.

Ann smiled wiping a tear from the corner of her eye, remembering him as a small boy climbing upon her knee to coax her into giving him sweetmeats, or his favourite Lancashire toffee which was filled with butter and treacle and sugar that stuck to his teeth. Ann made it to her own special recipe guarding her secret even from Cook who was a rival for Master Adam's affections. He had been such a lovely child.

Discounting Ann's theory as arrant nonsense but still not being offended by the suggestion, Sarah stood to her feet, smoothing her silken skirts and going briskly to the bell pull. She was now feeling full of vitality, making a mock of Doctor Hardcastle's prognosis. In the beginning she had felt poorly but now she was fighting fit and ready to tackle the problems that beset Josiah.

Jane came at her summons, red-eyed and pale causing Sarah to smile inwardly. The girl awoke in her echoes of her own youth.

"Jane, I want you to take me to see your brother."

"Me brother? Our Joe? Nay, Madam, you don't want to see our Joe, nay . . ."

Sarah smiled but assured Jane of her determination to see Joe Marsden with or without Jane's help, causing Jane to have a clear vision of Joe actually attacking Mrs Ayesthorpe should she travel to the dwellings alone.

"I'll take you then, but I have to tell you he's no good. No good to no one."

"We'll see," Sarah said.

Sarah knew about the dwellings, had seen them, but from a distance, she had never drifted down into those warrens, never let her dainty feet step along those un-paved highways with their mounds of manure and offal, the rivulets of filth running from overfilled cesspits, of piles of waste and refuse piled high to make tenements for rats.

In the centre of the courtyard was one stand pipe, which according to the plate instructions, would be turned on for twenty minutes once a day. There had to be two hundred men, women and children living in this court, how could they draw enough water for their daily needs?

Sarah had been poor as a child, knew poverty from first-hand experience but compared to this, her poverty was nothing. Their home had been in a country district, the air was fresh and pure, there had not been the stink rising from the very gutters, falling from the air in a soot-blackened pall, drifting in from the polluted river.

For a moment she reeled, found herself up against a wall trying not to retch into her handkerchief.

105

"My son lived here!" she mumbled, clasping Jane's hand in her own, "my son who was so used to the very best. God save us all, Mammy can you see it?"

"Are you all right, Madam, oh I knew I shouldn't never have brung you here."

"I'm all right, just give me a moment."

No wonder the cholera epidemic of 1832 had gained such momentum killing nearly a thousand people. This place and places like it had to be a breeding ground for any pestilence.

"Come, I am all right now. Hold my arm Jinny, tightly."

Carefully and gently she led her mistress to the building where her son had once lived and where Jane's brother and his wife and children occupied the cheapest room. The cellar.

The horror within was if anything equal to that upon the streets. The earthen floor was wet and dark, the mud seeping into Sarah's hand-made boots.

One candle burned casting elongated shadows, making phantoms of those within. Of Ellie upon the poor bed covered with old sacks that stank of mould. Two children huddled by her side, their heads against the outrageous swell of her belly.

The tea chest that had at one time served as a spare seat had been broken up long since and burned for firewood. There was nothing in that room save the poor bed, no plate, nor food, nor scrap enough to feed a not too hungry mouse.

"It's Madam come to see you our Joe," Jane murmured.

"Oh," Joe said standing. He was a small skeleton of a man but in the bad light Sarah could discern no feature, either of him or his wife and children. All their faces, as was hers and Jane's, pale voids in the dim darkness of this hole, and hole was what it was as far as Sarah could tell.

"And what do the fine Mrs Ayesthorpe want wi' the likes of us?" Joe sneered.

"I am not the *fine* Mrs Ayesthorpe, Joe Marsden, I am just *plain* Sarah Ayesthorpe."

She waited but nothing more was said, and Joe sank wearily onto the bed. The man was clemmed and without spirit.

"And I'll tell you what I want. I want you to gather your so called committee together and arrange a meeting, anywhere you name will suit as a venue."

"So the master will talk to us eh?"

"No. The master shan't but I shall."

Jane gasped but whether at Joe's expletive or at her mistress's statement no one knew.

"T'int woman's business," Joe argued. "They won't want to gather no where to meet no woman, tis the master we as after."

"Then you'll all end up in a pauper's grave."

"Dear God," Ellie cried fearfully.

"I am sorry, Mrs Marsden, but you must all be realistic. You have grievances, my husband thinks you have none. Trade has been bad and he made some cuts. Rightly or wrongly I cannot say. There are two sides to every coin and I am willing to hear yours just as I have heard his, and to act as an impartial middleman and to . . ."

"Impartial, you ain't impartial, you cannot be, not living in fancy high style you is . . ."

"I, I," cried Sarah, she was feeling well and truly ill now, wanting to vomit and afraid less should she do so it would be taken as a sign of her disgust by these people. The effort to stem the turbulent waves inside her made her appear impatient in her hysteria.

"I have known hunger myself. I know what it's like, the ache, the pain, the constant headaches, the inability to think and hope. I am you inside, because I am married to an owner doesn't make me different from you. Nor does it allow me to forget. My father was a hand loom weaver, my mother was murdered at Peterloo. Dear God, man, can you not see, I am all you have."

Jane saw her stagger slightly, knew the cause as her brother and his wife did not, and rushed to her side, put her arms around her waist to give her as much support as she could, willing all her young strength to flood into Sarah.

The silence was long, a stillness descended over all, the children barely moved. Ellie longed to cry, "aye, aye, go Joe, run and see if you cannot put an end to our woes through this little woman," but she dared not speak, dared not incite Joe's wrath.

"All right, Sarah Ayesthorpe, I'll take your plea to the committee, I can do no more nor will I, neither recommending for or against, will that do ee?"

"Yes Joe," Sarah said on a sigh, "that'll do."

The strike committee met at their usual office which was on the corner of Withy Grove and Shudehill. An ill-kempt pale thin band of men, two badly crippled by rickets causing them to be bow-legged. All looked to be in need of a decent meal and none as yet had gone onto poor relief which was the last resort for the desperate.

They listened silently to Joe, but as he had told Sarah, he would not recommend one way or the other. They must all thrash the matter out, stating the pros and cons and coming to a unanimous decision.

Fred Atkinson was all for telling Sarah Ayesthorpe what she could do with her interference but Harry Shaw was all for holding a meeting with her.

108

"Sarah is fair and straight," he argued, causing the others to laugh and tease him.

"Sarah is it?"

"Never mind that!" he retorted. "She is fair, she never forgets her own. She never got as she could not speak to you. There's no one in the whole of this town can point a finger at Sarah Ayesthorpe. She's honest and she's kind. Now I'm no Pape, I'm no Christian either come to that, but did she or did she not start a school for Catholic children? Does she not go about doing good turns? So what harm can it do for us to place our grievances before her."

"That's it, our grievances are with the master not his wife," someone said, "would I listen to my missus telling me what to do? Nay, nor would any of you, so why should we think that Joss Ayesthorpe'll listen to his?"

"Look," Harry Shaw was for the suggestion, anything rather than clem his way to the grave. "Joss Ayesthorpe in't bothered how long we stay out. He's got plenty o' brass, he don't need to ever open them gates again. He can stay in his comfy little house, painting his pictures, reading his fancy bound books, driving in his carriage with Sarah at his side. He will never approach us, nor let us see him. Sarah isn't *only* a chance. Sarah is our *only* chance."

This swung the argument more or less in Shaw's favour, yet they could not agree unanimously. The main prejudice against Sarah was that she was a woman, and therefore was unlikely to have any influence over Joss Ayesthorpe. Had the young and comparatively inexperienced George Littlemoss, Junior have called the meeting, it would have been accepted without question.

They decided upon a show of hands, out of the six only two voted to refuse.

"And where we going to meet her," one of the losers

109

smirked, "on t'street corner?"

"Nay," Joe Marsden said. "I'll send word with our kid an' ask her to ask Sarah to find us somewhere, she'll know what to do better'n us."

Adam faced Sangster across the dark red tablecloth. Between them a dozen oyster shells and a three-quarters full bottle of champagne.

"You cannot be serious!" Sangster insisted.

"Oh but I am," replied Adam, watching with interest as the waiter cleared away the debris from their first course. "I don't wish to live in London. My roots and ties are all in the north."

"But you must have London as your main base, to be on hand for any eventuality. Whoever heard of a successful artist living in Manchester!"

"I shall be the first," Adam said, filling his glass gaily. Sangster saw this beautiful talent, this sad but devastatingly attractive young man slipping through his fingers, escaping forever from the tiny bowl of society in which Sangster had taught him to swim.

He pondered his argument some long time, all the silky words of persuasion suitable for a dozen other people would bear no fruit if used upon Adam. Flattery meant nothing to him, adulation Sangster suspected, bored him. Women were only a source of physical delight, as one had been a willing victim to the artist's charm had confessed to Sangster.

"I do not think he has any soul, it's all in his art, for a few hours he is yours and then nothing."

Yet it was this very elusiveness that caused the women to pursue him even more. Titled ladies, married or widowed, since well brought up ladies were supposedly out of his reach, at least in theory. Anyway, Adam liked his women mature and experienced; shy blushing virgins he totally ignored.

110

Having thought about the question, Sangster decided to attack honestly and he hoped sincerely, the root cause of the problem.

"Isn't it time you cut yourself away from your mother," he said. There was no visible anger from Adam, but he took his time in replying, taking a long sip from a glass filled with a sparkling blond champagne.

"Why should I? Besides it isn't only Mama, it's the whole of the northern environment."

"Filth," Sangster said, "smoke, poverty . . . "

"Poverty is everywhere, just a moment from here and I could show you poverty that would make you sweat blood. I see other things, I see those delightful meadows over by Greenheys, where rumour has it I was conceived. About ten miles from my parents' home they own a small house beyond Oldham. There is nothing up there, just the moors and the curlews."

"You can go for a short rest, have a week or two . . . "

"No, I can't work here. I'll go home and I'll work, then I'll come back and if all the aforesaid isn't enough for you I shall tell you that I have a desperate need to frequently see the only perfect person I know, and if that makes you see me as a mama's boy then that's too bad because that, my dear friend, is how it is, and how I want it to be."

Sarah rented a Methodist Sunday school room for the meeting, took Jane with her and distributed a small amount of bread and cheese and cups of tea to the delegates, though stressing categorically that the alms were in no way to be taken as a bribe.

The men ate in silence, now and again shifting on their hard-backed chairs, surreptitiously watching the little woman who stood quietly by the window that looked down to the street.

She had not dressed down to them, on the contrary she

111

was splendidly attired in a pale violet gown of silk that emphasized the colour of her eyes. She wore little white lace mittens and carried a parasol. Standing so still and silent she might have been an exquisite doll in a toy maker's window. Indeed, a lady in miniature.

"We are right now, Mrs Ayesthorpe," Harry Shaw took it upon himself to make the announcement. Sarah took her seat before them.

"As I understand the matter, my husband cut your hours but wanted more production. So we have reduced hours, a loss of earnings but increased production. This was an action taken because of poor trade, as a means of not losing too much on the profit margin. Profit is important because it will enable better machinery to be bought and to carry out improvements in factory conditions."

"And to keep him in comfort," someone rasped, but was immediately told to shut up by the others.

"You are right. Naturally increased profit provides comfort for us. I accept that, but you all know my husband is a fair man. He is a man of liberal tendencies and works constantly for the Free Trade movement because he knows this is the only way that we shall prosper, and I do mean *all*. However, that is by the way, what do you want to end the strike?'

"No short hours and two shillings a week more."

"Two shillings a week more, that is a lot of money, especially when trade is bad."

Fred Atkinson stood to his feet, urging the others to do likewise. He could not see any sense in discussing their grievances with Sarah no matter how sincere she might be.

"We came here to talk about the problem," Sarah said, "if I am not allowed to state an opinion then there seems little point in continuing," she paused, and then said sharply, "sit down!"

Astonished by the anger he had ignited in the little woman before him, Fred Atkinson took his seat, aware of the slight titter that came from his colleagues.

"Would you go back if full pay and normal hours were offered?"

Their refusal was unanimous. Sarah looked at each man, she felt suddenly proud of them, at last it appeared that workers were beginning to unite against the unscrupulous methods of some of the masters though she felt it a pity that they had risen up against Josiah.

That she knew both sides of the coin inclined her towards the men. After all Adam had left Josiah and Lucy quite a lot of money. They, she and Josiah, owned their own home, they owned the house up on the moors and Josiah had made a splendid profit from the sale of the Oldham mill. He owned the large warehouse and the adjacent factory on High Street. They had no debts to speak of, it would not then beggar them to give the men what they wanted. However, she did recall Josiah saying something about it being wrong to subsidize a business, that each section most profitably support itself otherwise it was no use. Sarah did not understand the intricate world of finance, all she saw was that these men and many others were near starvation point, whereas she and Josiah were quite comfortably off.

"Right," she said, "this is my offer . . . "

"You in't in no position to offer owt," Fred Atkinson over his earlier embarrassment said. "It's fer master to say."

"If you consider what I am about to say and we come to some form of agreement then I shall present this to my husband for his decision. He might reject it, but then again he might not, it's a chance but what else is there for you?"

"Aye, aye, leave her be," Joe Marsden said, "let's see if owt can be done."

Sarah presented her offer; back on full time for one month in order to complete the orders awaiting manufacture. After a month a shilling a week more.

The men looked at one another, shuffling their feet and seeing their obvious distress, Sarah told them they should, of course, go and discuss it amongst themselves.

It would mean their taking the decision on behalf of their fellow workers because she could not, until she had presented the plan to her husband, allow them to put it to them first.

In single file they shambled out of the room, a tired ragged bunch of men almost beaten into the ground but by no means bowed.

Sarah leaned back in her chair, she felt exhausted, and taken over by lassitude. It appeared that the sudden burst of energy that had taken her over recently was fast fading.

As if sensing her exhaustion Jane brought her mistress a cup of tea. She had been sitting in the far corner of the room in awe of the manner in which Sarah had faced the strike committee, as she later told Dick, she weren't afraid of them fellows, rough as their appearance had to be to her. Mrs Ayesthorpe had the courage of a bantam cock.

Josiah, however, was furious with Sarah. His anger was not without some justification for Sarah had specifically been ordered to rest, and not only had she gone gallivanting to London with her erstwhile son, but had gone to the dwellings, a place rife with disease, and had later arranged a meeting with a hungry unruly mob of men who, in his opinion, were capable of any act of thuggery.

"Nay Joss," she murmured from her propped up

114

position in bed. "They would not have harmed me. They might feel obliged to strike you down or young George, but never me."

She was so pale, so delicate in appearance that his anger melted, leaving only minor irritation.

"Please consider their terms."

"Never. I have told you, I shall not allow a mob to dictate to me. You should not have interfered."

"At least think about it. Don't let my effort be so unworthy you cannot even look into it. It seems fair to me."

"Since when were you ever a financial expert any way," he said, but with a tender sort of sarcasm.

"One does not have to be a financial expert to see that they are starving slowly to death while Lucy—as a prime example—overeats to such an extent that she looks like a great white whale. Oh Josiah, have you seen those hovels, Joe Marsden's—my God I cannot call it a home —where have I been all these years, too busy to see what was happening." Her erubescent cheeks were a frightening contrast to the yellowness of her general complexion so that seeing her high agitation, Josiah went to her promising to look into the terms demanded by his operatives in order to end the strike. He would promise her anything just to calm her distress.

"And never underestimate what you have done. You have built a school, Sarah Ayesthorpe and do maintain it for poor children."

"It isn't enough!"

"It is more than most people have done."

"I'd like to pull those dwellings down with my own hands."

"Shush Sarah, please, rest think only pleasant thoughts. Please, for me?"

For him she pretended to acquiesce lying back in the

comfortable bed. If only she did not feel so enervated. Her exhaustion was rampant, there seemed no end to it, nothing she took gave her that feeling of having energy to burn that she had had when she had gone to London to be with her son.

Perhaps she had been wrong to walk out on Josiah while he was beseiged by troubles; to have been enjoying herself while he had been worried near death. This state then she thought might be God's way of punishing her for a selfish act. With the simple faith of a child she reached into her drawer and brought out the pale blue rosary beads that had belonged to her mother. She would pray very hard for forgiveness then perhaps God would make her better.

Maureen went to her mother's room the following mid-morning, entered quietly then sank onto her Mother's bed, her skirts and voluminous petticoats rustling loudly in the stillness.

Apart from good morning, Sarah said nothing. A visit from her daughter was a rare occurrence, it had been some time since her daughter had sought out her mother with eagerness, ready to confide and chat.

For some time Maureen merely sat, folding and un-folding her hands, watching the process with avid interest, then Sarah saw great tears fall like the first raindrops, becoming suddenly a torrent.

"Oh Maureen, my love, please do not cry. Come, you must stop this."

Maureen brushed aside her tears, eventually gaining control. Then she thrust a hand into the pocket upon her overdress, bringing forth a much crumpled sheet of paper, she thrust it into her mother's hand.

Sarah unfolded the sheet carefully, smoothing the thick paper before taking it up to read. It was a letter bearing the signature Charles Gray. It caused Sarah to start up, her heart to accelerate. Her first reaction to toss the letter aside with a sharp reprimand to her daughter, fading as she looked at Maureen and saw she must not do anything so cruel. Besides had she grown so old that she had forgotten the pain of first love. She herself had fallen in love at a very tender age so if her daughter was suffering only half as much as she had then she had to try to offer help and understanding and not instantly reject the girl.

"Are you certain that I should read this? A letter is a very personal thing, reading other people's letters seems to me to be like peeping at keyholes."

"I—I want you to read the letter Mama. Please."

Sarah read; the writing was quite clear, no need for her to query any point. It was a touching epistle, very sincere. If she had not known who had written it and was not prejudiced against him, she felt she would have liked the writer. There was nothing to dislike about him, and against her better judgement she was most careful to scrutinize some passage, a sentence, a word that she could misconstrue so to tell her daughter that the young man was no good.

He loved her! She looked up at Maureen seeing the tears fall from her lovely eyes. They were similar to Lucy's when she had been sixteen, but far more tender than Lucy's eyes had ever been, and far less flirtatious even when Maureen was in a giddy mood, the girl had a gentle nature.

The boy loved Maureen, her daughter, he loved her not passionately in youthful madness, not physically but deeply and what was worse it would appear that his love was of the permanent kind.

Slowly Sarah neatly folded the letter, handing it back to her daughter with a sigh.

117

"What can I say, Maureen. He obviously returns your love and, and—" it took all the strength Sarah possessed to say, "and he seems genuine and nice but you see, even were Papa and I to approve, his family would never consent to his marrying you. The Greys do not marry with—with people of our—" she shook her head, "people of *my* background. They never have done and they never will do so. I doubt you will ever forget each other or cease to love one another, but I am afraid there is no future for either of you together."

Maureen began to cry once more, burying her head in the satin quilt; inside of herself Sarah felt cold emptiness, a void at the bottom of which lay infinite sadness. Were her children for ever to be plagued by unhappiness had some vicious Diety laid a curse upon them; she would give everything she had to their persecutor in order that she herself might take on their miseries.

Tenderly she stroked her daughter's auburn head, murmuring words which though they were meant to offer comfort were quite useless.

"But if," Maureen began with a sudden spurt of optimism, "if the Greys agreed, would you and Papa—would you approve?"

"They never would do so, and supposition is a dangerous game, my darling." Sarah said in an effort to steer their conversation away from such a possibility. To even consider such an event would cause her so much pain; she could never approve nor agree, never contemplate having William Grey as her daughter's father-in-law.

"But if—" Maureen insisted.

"*If, if* the moon were made of silver, *if* the streets of London were really paved with gold, *if* is a cruel word."

"But *if* they did," Maureen was suddenly Grandfather Ayesthorpe, stubbornly refusing to be brushed aside.

"I do not know," Mother said, "I cannot say."

"You said Charles sounded nice and good. Mama you cannot hold him responsible for his father's ungracious behaviour."

"If only that were all," Sarah said, then realising she had gone too far shifted uncomfortably.

"There is more? Oh Mama what else, please, please tell me."

Mama sank back wearily, her daughter watched with anxiety as the colour fled from her already sallow skin, she watched horrified as Mama bit her lip almost to the point of making it bleed, her hands leaving her daughter's going now down beneath the bed sheet to rest upon the swell of her stomach.

"Aah," she gasped, "aah—"

"Mama, Mama what is it? Oh Mama, Mama!"

Sarah slid back, her eyes closing momentarily.

"Go, for the doctor—for Ann—for Papa," she managed, and then began to cry . . .

Doctor Hardcastle came at once, and shortly afterwards Doctor McLennon who had more modern methods arrived.

The house was hushed and silent as if every part, each corner were buried beneath roll upon roll of deep dark richly piled velvet.

Maureen sat with Papa in the study, she watched as he paced the small room, sometimes standing still twisting his hands and pulling off and then putting back onto his little finger, the heavy gold signet ring, the ring that Mama had bought him for their last wedding anniversary. Twenty years, twenty long years since they had said their vows at the Old Church, he resentfully, every word being torn from him and her, little Sarah, fifteen years old, trembling and afraid.

He began to pace again, raking his hands through his hair in an attempt to take his mind off from what was happening upstairs.

He had gone to the factory to think upon his problems, to bring together the twin evils of his pride and resentment against, as he saw it, the total betrayal of his labour force; to thrash them within his mind in order to come to a decision as to whether or not he could possibly accept their demands. To have to accept these demands demanded a lot from him, perhaps too much. Josiah never had done a *volte-face* willingly.

There were paid guards about the factory, protecting it from any possible attack by the hungry mob. Upon one corner a group of men clustered, not a large threatening mob, more a collection of human debris on whose skeletal form hung patched grubby clothing.

One man looked better fed than the others and as Josiah neared them—though cautiously crossing to the other side of the street—he saw that it was his father-in-law. Sam Ogden. The man he had taken into his home, fed and kept, when infirmity drove him from work.

Bitterness swamped him, each and every one of them strove to snap at his hand. His beautiful daughter, his melancholic son, his workers and now the arch-traitor his own father-in-law. Sam Ogden. Though he had known all along that Sam was a Chartist (since most men of worth had a detailed list of those belonging to the Organization) he had never told Sarah. Sarah—little Sarah he thought with a rush of feeling—did no more approve of Charterism than she would of Atheism.

Inside the factory all was still. It smelt of disuse of grease gone bad, rank and stale.

It was ghostly, the mighty looms, the very latest money could purchase grim and ugly in their idleness.

A surge ran through him, there was something beautiful in their motion, in the clatter of the shuttle as it dashed backwards and forwards threading the tiny fibres that eventually became bolts of one of the most incredibly beautiful of clothes, rich and sumptuous, warm and comforting.

As a young man he had avoided going into any of the mills, loathing the noise and atmosphere of dampness, preferring the peaceful dignity of the warehouses where great piles of dyed and finished rolls of cloth in a myriad of colour lay pile upon pile.

Now the looms were still and strangely no longer beautiful; weird and dusty, inanimate objects wasting away, almost like the men shuffling their feet upon the grim street corners. It was difficult for him not to draw this analogy for, despite his fairness as an employer, it was always as the partnership of men and machine that he saw his employees, not at the very depth of him did he see machine and man as separate entities.

The stillness of the factory acted as an echo chamber, the sounds of his feet upon the floor of the mill a hollow unfriendly sound.

Another sound now joined the one of his walking, voices echoing up to him from the ground floor; an excited hysterical voice belonging to an irate female, who in all probability was arguing with one of the factory guards. He thought of ignoring the fracas and was about to go down into his office when suddenly the noise of someone running up the stairs caused him to pause and then . . .

"Master Josiah, Master Josiah!"

But he had ceased to be Master Josiah on the death of his father he had become Mr Ayesthorpe, so who would call him Master Josiah, only someone who did not know him very well.

For a moment Josiah considered hiding himself in one

121

of the other rooms, then almost laughing he turned in the direction of the caller and let them know his whereabouts.

In moments, Ann was in the room, she was wearing her cap and apron, having not paused to remove them to put on outside clothing, her cheeks were flushed, her eyes wild in her frightened face.

Stiffly he faced her, cold irrational terror flooding into his veins.

"Come home, Master Josiah," she sobbed, "come home—Sarah," she said familiarly, "Sarah is having the baby."

Having the baby, how could Sarah be having the baby, it was much too soon, but it was an all too familiar pattern . . .

Never would he forget the nightmarish journey home. Ann sobbing by his side, the coach swaying as Ernest cracked is whip so that the horses would gallop. Now all they could do was wait. It occurred to him that he should have stopped to inform Sarah's father to let him accompany them back to Newton. All thoughts of Sam Ogden, the mill, his workers, had fled from his mind at Ann's news, but now recalling Sam he rang for Ernest.

"He's back sir," Ernest said, then quietly whispering. "He's sat on the stairs."

Sam Ogden old and bent was sitting in the very middle of the staircase, his rough large gnarled hands clasped together as if in prayer.

"Father," Josiah began . . .

Sam's soft eyes met his, then with contempt the old man looked away. Seeing no sense in beginning an argument Josiah went back into the study. His daughter was sitting in a high-backed chair, her hands tightly clasped around the arm, her features taut and frightened.

Somewhere above a door opened, then closed softly.

Maureen and Josiah went out into the hallway together. Sam had stood and was looking upwards.

Doctor Hardcastle was coming down the stairs, as he passed Sam the doctor put an arm around him, it seemed to Josiah a gesture of consolation. His stomach did a turn around, he went towards the edge of the stairway, putting his arm around the post for support.

As Doctor Hardcastle reached the bottom stair he looked up at Josiah's from beneath his bushy eyebrows, there was a wetness about his eyes that forewarned disaster. Slowly he shook his grey head.

"I'm sorry lad," he said.

"It's all right, I did not think the child could survive," said Josiah with a spurt of optimism which he pretended in an effort to push aside the torturous truth.

Doctor Hardcastle put his hand on Josiah's shoulder, pressing down heavily.

"Josiah, let someone fetch a priest for Sarah."

Angrily Josiah shook the doctor's hands off him, then mounted the stairs three at a time, running and throwing himself into the room that he had shared with his wife.

Adam Ayesthorpe left the coach and taking up his hand luggage swept up Market Street with an air of one who delighted in the joys of living.

The vast pall of smoke that hung permanently over the town was interspersed with sunshine—here and there the sun found a corner to bask, and it was on these warm corners that the jobless gathered; the matchsellers, the pamphleteers all watching his progress with a peculiar avidity, perhaps he thought, envying him his brisk agility.

He would stay at the dwellings for a while. Contrarily to what a lot of people thought Adam was reasonably happy in his room there. There was companionship to be found in the grim building, though he realized he would have to move to a new address, perhaps purchase a small house not too far from town maybe on Grosvenor Street, or near Plymouth Grove. Whatever else it was good to be home and to be quite positive that he had made the right decision.

The room had a long neglected air about it. Dust and grime covered the meagre furniture, the room smelling of mustiness; in his excitement at going away he had forgotten to ask someone to look after his room, to give the occasional dust and lighting the odd fire; something they would automatically do for any of the other neighbours but not for Master Adam because no matter how hard he tried they did not consider him as one of them.

After removing his new clothes, a grey coat and fawn trousers that he wore with a red silk waistcoat, and carefully unpinning the deep red rose from his button hole and putting it in a cup of water, he changed into his old painting clothes. They were very damp with mould growing here and there and he smiled as he imagined Mama's horror at such a state of affairs. Then he began in earnest to put his home in order.

In no time at all he had everything in comfortable shape, with a fire crackling brightly in the grate, then after going to the corner shop to purchase some food, he soon had a pan over the flames in which a thick slice of bacon aromatically sizzled. He cut a thick slice from the crusty loaf and spread it thickly with butter, mashed the tea and was almost ready to tackle with relish the plain but wholesome food when he was surprised by someone knocking at the door.

At his 'come in' he was even more surprised to see his cousin George Littlemoss. Adam quite liked George, though he considered him something of a dull fellow. Nevertheless George had been the one in the family to

124

keep in touch with Adam, and more especially to bring him treats when he had been short of money, so that Adam now made a mental note to invite George to dine with him one evening.

However, there was a subtle difference about George, a still paleness that had in it acres of pity. Ignoring the feeling of unease that feathered along his vetebrae Adam smiled his rare smile, the one that stopped hearts.

"What's the matter George, why so glum?"

"You don't know," George did not ask the question but sadly stated the obvious. He knew enough about Adam to know that his cousin would not smile for a very long time, if ever again.

"Don't know what? Come on, Georgie, out with it. Nothing can be *that* bad."

What to say. How to say the words that would destroy Adam Ayesthorpe. Should he say Aunt Sarah, or your mother. To say Aunt Sarah perhaps may momentarily make Adam think he was speaking of someone else. He could not just say, Sarah.

"Adam, your mother is dead."

Incredulously Adam stared at him, his mouth opened, his body so still that George thought he had been struck by some strange malady. He could hear himself giving the details of the event that had taken place two days ago. Slowly life returned to Adam, a grey haggardness came into his face, his eyes were bitter hard amethysts, his mouth twisting with murderous fury, then he was gone, running from the room, his feet thudding loudly on the worn wooden stairs.

Cautiously George, heavy-hearted, removed Adam's supper from the fire, then, after closing the door fast behind him, he too descended the stairs. He had come to seek out his cousin in his father's splendid coach, this had now brought out crowds of dirty people, clustering

125

around, fingering the fine highly polished door, touching the wheels, being watched with a full mixture of contempt, fear and anger by the coachman.

George pushed his way through the crowd but it was not difficult, for at his approach the mass of people parted, making a path from the door of the dwelling to the coach. For a moment he thought they might attack him, but they merely stood silently looking at him, their expressionless faces giving no clue to their mood, or if indeed they did resent him.

"Did you see which way Master Adam went?" he shouted up to his coachman, before the man could reply someone in the crowd called.

"Aye right up to the top of town, he be running all the way to Newton, I'll wager."

The mob murmured their agreement to this statement so George ordered his driver to take him up Oldham Road, keeping a watch out for Master Adam on the way.

Adam indeed was running to the elegant house at Newton. People stopped and stared at him, some recognizing his long lean-limbed frame and knowing the reason for his haste turned away compassionately.

For his part he was unaware of any person, or even of himself, or the thud of an overactive heart, or the pain at the back of his legs. He was out of town now, by sweet meadows, leaving behind the smoky grimness of the town, even these he did not see as he strove to reach his mother's home.

A carriage pulled abreast of him, George had to call several times before Adam stopped, then seeing George he lurched brokenly towards the transport, and as the door opened threw himself down upon the floor where he lay gasping for breath, managing only to choke. "Go—go!"

George helped Adam onto the seat, his clothes were

soaked, with sweat clinging to him wetly, his hair plastered about his forehead.

"You poor bloody fool," George whispered, going to the box beneath the opposite seat and taking out a flask of brandy.

Fortified by taking long measured sips of the potent spirit he said! "I'm going to kill that bastard."

His father was in the study in the company of Maureen. Adam did not see the haggard face, the tortured eyes, he saw only him, the man who had without doubt murdered his mother as surely as if he had put his hands about her tiny throat and choked her to death.

Both father and daughter looked up, and then drew closer together at the apparition in the doorway.

"You murderer," Adam cried, then lunging like a drunk across the room he pushed aside his sister, took his father by the lapel, shook him and then when Josiah was too weak or so uncaring he did not wish to resist he struck him a violent blow that caused the blood to spurt from his nose, the sight of blood, the sound of tortured flesh seemed only to increase rather than calm his violence but something, someone was making his castigation of Josiah difficult, someone holding on to his back and legs, clinging to his shoulders and screams and cries that competed with the vitriol that was spilling from his mouth.

"You murdered her, you murdered my mother!"

There was more hindrance now, his father had slumped weakly to the floor but he could not bend to pull him to his feet to attack him again.

Maureen who had been clinging to her brother's back released her hold on him to fall beside her father, taking his head into her lap caressingly.

"Nay lad, tha'll not strike thy father," someone said.

127

Turning Adam saw he was now firmly held by not only Ernest but Grandfather Ogden, himself a shadow of his former self.

Ann the housekeeper, who had hugged and cuddled him when he had been a small child was openly sobbing in the doorway, twisting her large white apron in front of her as if she were ringing it out.

"Ann?" he cried a question. The old woman shook her head from side to side, then let her gaze go up the stairs all the while biting her lips.

Adam went to move forward but his grandfather and the coachman still had his arms fastened by his side.

"I must go to her," he said. Mutely Sam Ogden released his hold on Adam, nodding for Ernest to do likewise.

As the cynosure for all eyes Adam crossed the silent room, pausing only to put a gentle hand upon Ann's shoulders as if to reassure her that his violence had dissipated.

Slowly, heavily as if the weight of the world had fallen onto his shoulders, he climbed the staircase.

She was not dead, he thought, on seeing her, but the victim of some strange malady that had sent her into a deep coma, from which she would shortly recover. It would be like the fairy tale. She was the sleeping princess and a kiss from him would revive her.

A feel of her cheek though quickly dispelled this momentary illusion. Weakly he sank onto the chair beside her coffin, tears like flooding rivers falling from his eyes.

"Oh Mama, Mama, how am I going to live without you. How can I survive in a world that does not have your smile, you know that everything—good or bad—I have done for you."

It went dark, and still he sat beside her, talking to her softly, asking innumerable questions of her who could give no reply.

"You left me once before and I almost died, I want to die now, Mama."

Eventually someone entered the room, causing Adam to turn violently, if it was him, his father come to take him away from her again, he knew that this time the blow would be final and positive. But it was not Josiah it was Ann, coming to stand by his side, putting her arm around him after placing a candelabrum on the bureau by the door.

"Come now Adam, some people have come to pay their last respects. Come downstairs."

"When I leave this room I leave the house," he said. Then because she moaned sadly he asked her about the funeral arrangements. It would be tomorrow, at St Patrick's Livesey Street.

"Your father sent word to London, Adam, someone's probably searching for you even now."

Adam did not reply but turned his gaze to Sarah. It would be for the last time, greedily he drank of her, those pale cheeks, the dark cluster of curls so lovingly arranged, the jet lashes so very very long.

"She looks like a little girl", he said.

"Aye just like she did when first I saw her. A skinned rabbit of a thing. Eh, Adam, I loved her so much."

The people came in droves, they poured from the weeping sore that was Ancoats in a steady silent mass. Grim-faced men, their women beside them, their heads covered by dark woollen shawls. They came from the dwellings, from courts and warrens, from Little Ireland, a steady seeming never-ending stream of poor.

A visiting Frenchman paused to enquire the reason,

feeling somewhat fearfully that the crowd be bent upon revolution.

"Nay lad," someone told him, "they'll be going to Sarah's funeral."

St Patrick's Church was set amidst the green fields of Livesey Street, between St George's Road and Oldham Road. It was a proud cruciform shaped edifice with a clock tower, and against the law of the land, it had bells.

Here the crowds divided, those not of the faith stood outside in quiet groups, while the others, mostly Irish, went inside. Within it was almost full, the galleries swelling with people.

At the front of the church in the first pew upon the right-hand side was Josiah Ayesthorpe, his daughter beside him, her arm through his, the grip more supportive than it would seem, and by her side Sam, Sarah's father.

These three were then alone, behind them was Lucy, George and their two sons, then in the pew behind them was gathered the Ayesthorpe servants, these had been given a choice of attending since it would be a Catholic Mass, none had declined but Jane looked apprehensively about her and though she sensed deep within herself that Mrs Ayesthorpe, even from her coffin, would protect her from harm, nonetheless she could not help the ripple of fear that ran over her as a dark clad nun looked at her with gentle curiosity.

In the front pew upon the opposite side of the church stood Sarah's son. His alienation a startling thing, that even with the solemnity of the occasion was whispered about, as was his father's angry black eye.

Behind Adam was Sarah's partner in the school venture, Mr Harrop and his sister, together with a group of older children. Mr Harrop seemed to be in remarkable control but his sister was weeping copiously.

The church was now crammed and was overly warm, the smell of the poor rising in a sickening wave, causing Lucy to wish she had taken a small dose of laudanum to sooth her nerves.

"I'm not going to be getting up and down," she rasped. "I'm not a Papist, I'm going to sit here and that will have to do."

George Littlemoss made no reply, he had anyway barely heard what she had said, he seldom listened to Lucy these days; he was thinking about the race meeting he had intended going to with his friend Will Grey, however Lucy had insisted he attend the funeral; not that he had not liked Sarah, indeed he had liked her enormously but she was dead, that was all there was to it, regret it as he might there was little he could do about it.

Father Hearne entered, behind Lucy all stood. Sam stood but Josiah even though aided by Maureen was unable to do so. Maureen relinquished her hold upon him so that he could slump into his seat, his head buried in his hands.

Lucy and George remained sitting, she burying her face in her lavender-scented handkerchief. To her consternation Frank and George were standing, angrily she tugged at the latter's coat but for her trouble received a damning look of such fury she let her hand fall weakly to her side.

George, and to a lesser degree her younger son Frank, were so disagreeable to her these days. They never behaved to her as Adam had behaved towards Sarah; he had really loved his mother, no one could dispute that. Automatically her eyes went to Sarah's son. He stood so tall and erect, so like Josiah when he had been that age, yet Adam was warmer than Joss had ever been; her brother could be so hard, so narrow. Adam had Sarah's warm blood in his veins.

131

"Maureen Bridget," the priest was saying. Who was Maureen Bridget—then she knew—Sarah. Her mother had named her Sarah as she had been unable to remember her own name and Sarah she had become. Sarah for plainness that was why Dorothea Ayesthorpe had called her Sarah. Her own given names though were so lovely.

Lucy's eyes filled with tears, they multiplied and rolled endlessly. "Oh Sarah, now I have no one to talk to!"

Only the close family and friends clustered around the graveside, though some short distance away the crowd still gathered silently.

Adam still maintained his distance, standing to the right of Father Hearne, away from his father. His distance censure enough.

Lucy pondered upon the advisability of asking Mr Harrop and his sister to the cold buffet she had prepared at the Newton house. After all they were close—had been close friends of Sarah's—but then again it was common gossip that Mr Harrop had been in love with Sarah. Josiah had always teased her about it and if there was one thing guaranteed to anger Sarah, it had been to tease her about Mr Harrop.

Josiah's tossing a bouquet of dark crimson roses into the deep gaping hole brought Lucy suddenly from her reverie.

Father and son were facing each other for the first time that day, their eyes meeting and holding, until Adam turned away.

Everyone had departed, the sky turned scarlet at sunset and still he stood, alone, though not alone. She was there, beneath a coverlet of exquisite floral tributes. He had memorized every name of the senders; people he did not know, people whom he did. Quakers, Wesleyans, Anglicans, business people, shop owners, teachers and

132

clerics, an assortment of people, how had she known so many, what did she do with her time that she had over the years come into contact with such a mixed crowd. He would probably never know.

Gone he thought, feeling that now he was completely alone. The family, his family meant little to him, regretfully not even Grandfather Ogden. His world had been Mama and to a lesser extent Grandfather Ayesthorpe, now they had both gone.

Dusk was falling before he eventually managed to gain sufficient courage to leave her. Once he left the graveside he doubted very much that he would ever come back again.

It would be Josiah who would erect the stone, who would direct the mason on what to chip out, what to say, looking at it he felt he would be remined only of his father rather than her.

"Goodbye Mama," he murmured, then turning he walked away. He was empty.

Six

"Can you not see it, *fach*, the sense of it? Four shillings a day I'll be getting, four shillings a day, much more than I can ever earn in that smelly old foundry."

"Four shillings a day to spend in the company grog shop!"

"There is unfair you are, Jinny Marsden, for when have I ever spent my money on drink?"

Jane knew the answer, was aware also that she was being unreasonable. The reality was that she was afraid that if he once went away he would never come back again; that he would meet someone else and forget all about her and their plans.

"All I have to offer is a strong back, I am not clever enough to invent machinery, or paint fancy pictures," Dick argued. "But I can dig and if I work on the railroad for at least a year we shall have enough money saved for our plans."

"They might not take you on!"

"Mick O'Grady has told me . . . "

"Humpf, him! Irish, you can't trust the Irish. They tell lies," mortified Jane heard herself say the words, feeling pangs of conscience remembering her late beloved mistress in her grave one long month.

Dick made no other comment, his exasperated sigh enough of a statement.

A gust of wind pushed up Oldham Road, bringing with it a veil of black smoke that bit savagely into their eyes and lungs; a shower of smutty flakes fluttering down with all the elegance and grace normally associated with flakes of snow.

"There is difficult you can be," Dick's firm tone caused her to look up suddenly, this same firmness was carried on into his face, marring his usual bland though pleasant features so that these became hard and resolute, proving what she already knew, that she had indeed gone too far. Yet how could she extricate herself. Jinny Marsden was equally as stubborn as the Welshman she had come to love. In the past she had been over confident certain that his love for her was eternal and would last their lifetime, this fresh idea he had had for making money quickly though had shaken her confidence. She was as vulnerable as the next person, haunted by the realism that love did not necessarily last forever. Perhaps, too, she thought, this was his excuse to leave town, never again to return, leaving her to a future that might become an echo of Letitia's; a life of spinsterhood, enlivened only by a romantic attachment to her master.

"Well go then," she said, "an' see if I care."

For a moment he looked at her, then turning on his heels, he walked briskly away. Hands in pockets, his shoulders erect he walked with a lightness that was hurtful. Hugging her shawl to her against the smoke filled chill wind she watched him, some inner sense conveying the fact that he would not turn to look at her, and that once he turned the corner into Ancoats Street she would never see him again.

Casting her pride to the wind she ran after him, when she came alongside she said nothing, merely keeping pace at his side. He was silent for so long that she came to think that indeed he had planned it all so that he could extricate himself from their unofficial engagement, then when she had given up all hope, he took her hand, holding it firmly in his large rough one.

"Please take care," she said, three days on, seeing him

135

on his way. "The work is hard and dangerous, they do say."

"Have no fear, *fach*, I shall be all right. I promise you."

George Littlemoss, Junior had to confess to himself that Uncle Josiah was not as bad as he had imagined he would be, especially since the last time he had seen him had been after Aunt Sarah's funeral. Then George had not given much chance for his uncle's survival. He had appeared thin and old and broken, the purple swollen flesh around his eyes making him appear as a burned-out pugilist. He also much to Maureen's concern, had consumed enormous quantities of brandy, morosely staring at the mourners while saying nothing.

George had stayed on after the others had departed, and after he had passed out, had helped Ernest to put his uncle to bed. Then there had been Maureen to console. Not only had she lost her mother at a critical stage in her life but she was watching her father sink into the dismal abyss of despair. He would not eat, but would drink brandy and smoke cigars. From the moment he awoke until he slid into a drink-induced oblivion.

However, things had changed. Sarah had been buried ten days and it would appear that Uncle Josiah had fully accepted the fact, or had he? George worried. Uncle Josiah was sober, quiet, less morose but different. He was cold, so very cold. His eyes no longer warm summer blue but as chilling as steel. He appeared not to be listening to his sister and did not bother to conceal his boredom.

For his own part George squirmed with embarrassment as his mother, with her usual lack of tact, demanded that Josiah either open the factory, at the same time making George a full partner, or sell the business to her husband.

136

This latter suggestion brought a dark flush to Uncle Josiah's pale cheeks but his voice when he spoke was cold and clipped. Aunt Sarah it would appear, had drained all the warmth from him, had taken it with her to protect from the chills of her damp grave.

"I would not sell your husband a bag of manure, Lucy," he spat, causing Lucy to gasp with such passion that George reached out to clasp her hand. Uncle Josiah looked now at George, there was no apology in the look but a slight softening.

"You have no right to speak that way about my husband."

"The firm of Ayesthorpe and Son will always remain Ayesthorpe and Son, or I shall disband it. I certainly would not let the man who owns the dwellings have anything to do with it.

George looked from Uncle Josiah to Mama, seeing her cheeks flush and her inability to meet her brother's gaze.

"Mama," he asked, "does Papa own the dwellings?"

Lucy shifted upon her seat, unwilling to give an answer. Her head was beginning to ache, it always began at the back of her skull creeping slowly until her whole head felt as if it were in a vice. She wanted to go home now, to her room, where the tiny bottle offered relief.

"Yes," Josiah said, seeing that Lucy would not answer. "He sits upon those rat holes waiting for the right time to pull them down, waiting only for the value of the land to climb sky high. I despise him for that. I am sorry, George, but that is how I am. The firm is for my son and . . ."

"*Your son! Your son!*" Lucy squealed, "your son doesn't want the factory or you," she said, then cruelly, "sometimes I don't believe he is *your* son."

Although George remonstrated with his mother,

Josiah said nothing. He went quickly across the room, lifted the lid of a silver box and took out a slim cigar. Mama would not be appeased, pouring out bitter words to her brother whose very impassivity made her even more angry.

"If Sarah were here she . . . " she screamed. At this her brother turned.

"If Sarah were here you would not dare to make so bold an accusation." Josiah spoke so coldly that Lucy shivered, she could never understand him or what Sarah had loved about him. He was so severe.

"My son will inherit my office," he repeated though with such confidence George wondered was his mind quite in order. "The time of play for him is over."

Lucy left shortly after in angry tears, her enormous skirts catching an ornament and sending it from the table onto the floor. The luxurious carpet softened the impact so that it did not shatter. George paused to pick it up and replace it.

"See your mother into her carriage then come back. I want to talk to you. *Alone*," stressed his uncle.

Lucy did not want him to stay but was so overwrought she did not argue with him too long, besides she was anxious to reach her room and the blessed relief that would be hers when she took the laudanum.

"I do not want you to think me unreasonable," Uncle Josiah said, when George returned. "I admire your work and many's the time I have wished you were my son, but you aren't. You're a Littlemoss and I can't hand over half of Ayesthorpe business to a Littlemoss. But there is something I will do for you," he paused to smile, a wintry smile that did not make his eyes sparkle, "but on a condition. An Ayesthorpe as my father would say, never does owt for nowt. Adam must take over the reins from me . . . "

138

Without wishing to be rude, George had to interrupt, had to make his uncle see that whatsoever else happened his son would never take over the business.

"He will, I shall make him. Be assured, George, one of these days it will be you and Adam."

"But I can't see how."

"No, I suppose you can't. However once Adam does take over," Uncle Josiah said confidently. "I will give you a thirty-five per cent share. Adam must have controlling interest, always. After him will come his son and so it will go on. My father dreamed of a dynasty and by God his dream will come true." Josiah inhaled deeply on his cigar, blowing a cloud of smoke up into the air, watching its spiralling course some time, as if the answer to all his problems was written there.

"Of course you might decide to start out on your own, and I would not dream of stopping you, though at the same time hoping you won't do so."

"I shan't. At least not in the immediate future. The factory is my life," George said emphatically. "Thirty-five per cent will have to do, but when do we go back into production. The terms Aunt Sarah arranged were not too bad."

"Give me time," Uncle Josiah said, "now I want you to do something in exchange for thirty-five per cent."

He met George's eyes, his nephew's eyes were of a tender pale brown shade, honest and kind, perhaps too kind for his own good.

"I want you to marry my daughter."

Incredulously George stared at his uncle, then there came a rush of joy that was too quickly swept away by a tide of acute depression that settled lumpily at the very base of his stomach.

"Maureen doesn't love me," he said, "she will never agree."

"Maureen will do as she is told." Josiah stated with an even fiercer conviction than when he had given assurances that Adam would enter the Ayesthorpe business.

"I take it you are not adverse to marrying her?"

George assured his uncle that nothing would give him greater pleasure than to have Maureen Ayesthorpe as his wife. His cousin was the most beautiful girl he had ever known, and she was most certainly the only woman who had teased his senses, distracting him from business.

Because he thought a good deal about her, he was too cautious to call it love, he had to try to explain as best he could that Maureen was in love with Charles Grey, without giving away the information that the lovers were indeed corresponding with alarming frequency.

"I know that she thinks she is in love with Grey. That is beside the point. She will never marry him. I would *never* allow it. On the other hand she is not made for spinsterhood. She needs a husband and children. As to love, well that will come in time and if it doesn't," Josiah shrugged, "it isn't the be all and end all of everything. Friendship and respect are sound substitutes."

"Why can't you let her marry Charles Grey, Uncle Joss? I know you don't get on with Sir William but Charles is not like him, I do assure you he is . . . "

"I don't give a damn what Charles is and is not. He may be a saint for all I care. Ayesthorpes do not marry Greys and I'll tell you why."

"I trust you," Uncle Josiah said later when he had told George the true reason for his empathy towards the Greys. "I trust you never to tell anyone. One day you might have to tell Maureen, I'd prefer it if it was more or less a matter of life and death."

George had turned a ghastly shade of white, so alarming a colour that his uncle went to a decanter and poured him a good measure of brandy.

"I feel so angry," he said, "angry and impotent too. Poor Aunt Sarah!"

"You can see now why it can never be. Sarah is at rest. I want that rest to be peaceful. It never could be were Maureen to marry the son of her mother's murderer."

There was a cluster of small elegant houses near Plymouth Grove. A terrace of three-storey late Georgian houses, access into which was made directly from the street.

The backs of the houses let out onto a square of lawn with a perimeter wall some thirty yards from the back door. A quiet elegant row of houses providing suitable abodes for lawyers, or those in a managerial position.

Adam chose to buy number three because he had sufficient funds to pay cash. This was the one and only criteria. His very emptiness made the normal consideration as to size, attractiveness and durability unnecessary.

It was here that Lucy saw him. She was accompanying the duchess upon an excursion into town and was both flattered and nervous. Although she had known Arabella as a girl, their social positions were now vastly different and not only this, but Arabella had retained her looks and her very presence was painful to Lucy, whose good looks had long since faded.

The sight of her nephew entering one of the terraced houses caused a gasp of anger to escape her, and so irritated was she by this glimpse of him that she, without prior consultation with Arabella, instructed the coachman to halt the pair of white horses that pulled Arabella's luxurious coach.

"Please excuse me," Lucy managed, gathering her skirts about her, "but I must speak with that young man."

141

Arabella lent forward to look at the man who had disquieted Lucy. He had, in the interim, gone into the house leaving a box upon the pavement while taking within several canvasses. However he had come out once more to retrieve the box before Lucy had reached them.

"Adam, Adam!" Lucy cried, "I would have a word with you."

He stopped, then after raising his hand in a graceful salutation he bent to retrieve the box, holding it high on his chest and giving his aunt the slightest of smiles.

"You wicked boy," Aunt Lucy gasped feeling breathless from the slight exertion of walking across the road at, for her, some speed.

"Aunt Lucy, how charming you look. What a fetching bonnet."

"Oh don't try to beguile me," she said, but with delight, feeling pleasure invading her anger.

"Come and look at my house," he coaxed softly. Lucy looked up at him, meeting his eyes and holding his glance, seeing too late the frown that came to mar the smoothness of his brow.

"Oh Aunt Lucy, what are you doing to yourself?" He asked compassionately. Too late she looked away, fretfully putting a hand over her mouth.

"You won't tell, Adam, promise you won't tell?"

Sadly he looked down at her. She was fat and unpretty a selfish, spoiled woman who he had seen was addicted to opium. She led a useless life and yet God, if indeed there was a God, had seen fit to call his mother to His side rather than this woman, who through boredom was slowly killing herself.

He wanted to counsel her, to persuade her to cease the habit, he would have done so had another not swept up to them, and sweep indeed she did.

She was incredibly lovely with her blonde curls and

fair complexion, her blue jacket and skirt an exact match for her large liquid eyes.

"Lucy," she lisped prettily.

"Arabella, I'm so sorry," Lucy said, relieved that Arabella's joining them had prevented Adam from further discussing her need of laudanum. He was Sarah's son, and like Sarah before him would not go telling tales to her husband.

"Have you met my nephew?" Lucy gushed, drawing Arabella closer.

"No."

Lucy performed the introduction, oblivious to the fact that the two strangers were studying each other with more care than a casual introduction would warrant.

Adam Ayesthorpe was like, and yet was not like, his father. He had Josiah's long leanness and the thick dark golden hair that would fall boyishly over his wide brow. He had his father's straight nose, but his mouth was softer, the lips equally as finely drawn as Josiah's but with a vague difference in the fullness of the lower. His eyes were not like Josiah's. Adam's eyes were the colour of trampled violets, sad but so very beautiful.

Arabella had to concede that the son was most certainly far more handsome than his father. She had always been attracted to Josiah, had desired him but these feelings were mild in comparison to how she felt looking at his son. A wild savage emotionalism ran riot through her. She felt it at the tip of her breasts, at her pulses, a throbbing pleasure that was hurting in its intensity, a sickness in her stomach and a weakness in her thighs.

Her eyes tangled with his and even though she saw the cynical raise of his left eyebrow she could not turn haughtily away.

Somehow they were making polite conversation, he was asking her how long she was staying in town and she

143

was telling him, the great gaps in their conversation Lucy filled.

"Show us your house then," Lucy said.

"No!" Arabella almost choked out the word. "I—I mean we must go, there is not time."

How Arabella got through the rest of the afternoon she would never know. Whatever had induced her anyway to ask this vacuous woman to accompany her in a saunter around the shops. They had long ceased to have anything in common.

Shop assistants came in for tongue lashings from her so that even Lucy became somewhat ashamed of being in her presence. Lucy could be an unreasonable customer with the rest but everyone fawned and grovelled over Arabella so that her fault finding was ludicrous.

As she snapped at those whose job it was to serve, Arabella's mind seethed, torturing her with the true facts of the matter.

These were that she was nineteen years older than Adam Ayesthorpe (she did not look it she knew, and she had grown fond of the salvish attentions of younger men) but of more import he was the son of *that* woman. The woman who had trapped and tricked Josiah Ayesthorpe and so taking him from her clutches. If she thought about that fact frequently enough then that would cool her ardour. It did not work.

The purchase of the house at Plymouth Crescent had all but beggared Adam. Now that he was settled within the walls of his very own home he took time out to consider his decision. For weeks now he had been living in a state of half awareness. To all he met he presented a façade of normality, but inside his head he had felt as though his brain were smothered within layers of cotton wool; for weeks he had been half alive, uncertain, unsure, looking at properties and only bothered over

144

whether he had enough money for the purchase.

To have spent all he had earned had been ludicrous because now, as his mourning softened, he could not see how he would ever earn more money. Certainly not by painting. He had a small book in which was written a long list of commissions won, a list of such variety many an aspiring artist would have considered murder just to own a quarter of the orders.

He could not paint anymore. He could not paint to order, though hunger had in the past driven him to this. He felt neither inspiration or need to work, inside there was nothing. Mama had taken with her his ambition and desperate desire to prove that he was better than his father at art, that his thoughts rode upon a far higher plane, but now there was no one person he cared about sufficiently to have to prove anything.

Seeing the humour he smiled, within this house lay his worldly goods, four blank canvasses, a goodly selection of oil paints, a bundle of clothing, a box of treasures. Slowly he went through the box turning over in his hands familiar items, a favourite book, a flat grey pebble stolen from the shore at Brighton where he and Mama had spent several weeks. Papa had been in London at the time and Maureen it was felt, was too young to travel so far. A bundle of letters tied with dark violet ribbon because it reminded him of the colour of Mama's eyes. Certain memories of the past called to him; it was a threatening call so that he must summon all his defences, meet the enemy and so brutally slay it.

These were his belongings, these and a bed, a table and a chair, and a well-worn cast-off rug, given to him by his cousin George.

There was gas lighting at the house but he owned no lamps to give an alternative more warming glow. He did not even possess any curtains, and for the moment could see no way of earning sufficient money to enable him to purchase the most basic of household goods.

He did not care; he was surviving that was all.

The rooms of the house had been freshly painted, though some of the colour schemes were not to his taste he could in this state of half aliveness tolerate sharing his life with them.

Sangster bombarded him with demanding, sometimes gently entreating letters, which he used to light the fire. One letter he received was not from Sangster but was a confused epistle from his sister. Apparently Papa had arranged a marriage for her with George Littlemoss. She did not want to marry her cousin, she was in love with some fellow called Grey. In the letter she implored Adam to help her, but Adam could not see how he could do so. Maureen had always been his father's favourite child, that had always been obvious—as had the fact that Mama had preferred him—he had not cared, such a thing did not matter. His sister and he had never been close, he quite liked her as he quite liked his cousins but he had no great sense of family feeling towards her.

What was strange was Papa insisting that Maureen make a loveless marriage, and one she obviously did not desire to make. As Maureen was just seventeen Josiah's haste would seem to be unneccessary. However, Adam could see no way of helping his sister, she would have to defy her father as he had done before her. Sadly he also threw this letter upon the fire.

Several days on someone hammering upon the brass door knocker disturbed the silence. Adam was laying upon his bed, his hands behind his head, letting his mind drift. With effort he rolled off the bed going from the room slowly and without bothering to put on his jacket. Something he much regretted when he opened the front door to find the Duchess of Livingstone upon his step.

"Your Grace," he mocked, the more so because of his own untidy appearance which was in vivid contrast to Arabella's elegance.

She had taken her carriage into town, after dismissing the driver she had taken a hackney coach out to Plymouth Grove, the art of discretion being second nature to her.

"You invited me to see your house," she said.

"No, my aunt asked you to look at my house," he said, then smiled to soften the remark. His smile was electrifying, no wonder he did not do it often. People would fall over in delight, she thought.

He stood back to allow her to proceed him into the house, cautiously she looked around her, the street was deserted, no one would observe her entrance. Quickly she stepped within. It was a little chilly after the mildness of the outdoors.

Seeing at once that the house was practically empty Arabella whirled around, a questioning expression upon her face.

"Out of funds," Adam replied nonchantly, "but I do believe I have a drop of port left and two glasses."

She sat upon the wooden chair while he sat upon the table, a glass of port in her gloved hand, apart from a carton of miscellaneous items there was nothing else in the room.

Fastidiously she glanced at the wooden floor with its layer of dust, then looking up caught his eyes upon her. He was amused by her disdain and her attempt to conceal it.

"I used to fancy myself in love with your father," she murmured, more for the need to say something than from a desire to confess.

"He used to fancy himself in love with you," he answered smoothly. Before she could say anything else a thought suddenly struck him, and he asked urgently. "Tell me does your brother have a son called Charles?"

Although she confirmed this fact to him Adam did not tell her the reason for his query. It did not matter anyway. If Papa would not allow Maureen to marry Charles Grey, since she had always been his favourite child, then even disliking his father as he did, he had to admit that Josiah must have a very good reason.

"I believe you paint," Arabella said. "Perhaps I could arrange some commissions for you."

Slowly Adam lowered himself from the table, thrusting his hands into his pockets.

"I have a bookful of commissions, love," he murmured going to look out of the window. "I am just not interested. Why did you come here?"

Arabella said nothing, not daring to tell the truth, that she found him irresistible. Flirtations she had had but they had been conducted according to the rules. She had only once chased a man, Adam's father, and that had resulted in his most harsh rejection of her. It had dented her confidence somewhat, although she had decided to pursue him once more; only his wife's death had prevented her arranging a meeting. However, on meeting his son all thoughts of Josiah had flown her mind.

"I had better leave," she said, standing now and taking up her parasol. He came across the room towards her causing such a trembling to invade her that she doubted her ability to walk away.

"You're very beautiful," he said softly. Becoming at once the older of the two. She felt like a young reckless girl again, yet one without the ability to flirt and to be in command and cruel.

"It was nice of you to call, I am only sorry that I could not make you more comfortable."

"You might have put on your jacket," she managed to

tease, then unable to meet the intense gaze of his violet eyes she looked down.

"I am sorry, you are right."

"Oh, I was only jesting."

Her gloves were oyster pink like her gown, as she raised her hand to touch a golden curl that rested upon her shoulder the hand brushed the white silk of Adam's flowing sleeved shirt; reluctant to leave the warmth of his skin beneath the material she let her hand linger.

In a moment Adam circled her hand in his, squeezing her fingers tightly. With surprise she looked up at him. When he did not smile there was a reminiscent severity about his features, but more, so much more. There was a lazy sensuality, a promise of pleasure.

His other free hand stretched out capturing her about the waist and drawing her close to him.

Her vast voluminous skirts and petticoats prevented her from feeling his body, causing her to be momentarily angry, her lips parted in a snarl of disgust at the sheer animal passion that was rushing headlong through her blood. He, as if only waiting for this sign seized her mouth within his own, kissing her with an intimacy that made mock of their short acquaintance.

"No! No!" She gasped when he released her mouth, to lay siege to the sensitive areas of neck and ear. Somehow her bonnet had become loosened and her curls, fell wantonly about her, her hair combs and clips scattering like so much debris onto the unclean floor.

"I want you," Adam said, looking down at her. Close too there were tiny wrinkles both beneath, and at the side of her eyes, yet they did not detract from her essential beauty. Her features were delicately formed so that she would always be beautiful and ageless.

His hand had found her breast and in its manipulation had released it from the layers of cloth so that even though it was protected from his searching gaze he could feel the delicate line and the puckering hardness of its centre. Contrarily she implored him to stop. Her mouth as well as her aroused breasts made mockery of her plea, but he prided himself upon being something of a gentleman. Abruptly he released her, she reeled a little, as if surprised.

He said, brutal in his honest "I want you. I do not wish to play stupid games."

Josiah Ayesthorpe—after carefully arranging the items upon his desk—rang for Ann.

She came quietly and with the strange sort of stillness that had descended over the house. Her eyes were slightly red-rimmed so that Josiah wished, not for the first time, that the others would stop their tears as he had had to; to catch sight of Ann or that little Marsden chit wiping away a tear only made him acutely aware of his aloneness.

"Sarah," he said abruptly, "left these gifts. I would rather you distributed them. These are for Letitia, these for Cook and surprisingly this brooch for that Marsden girl." Ann quietly collected the various pieces of jewellery, putting them carefully to rest in the large pocket at the front of her apron.

"She left you these things," Josiah pushed a small enamelled box towards Ann. It was designed as a pirate's chest with leather straps over its raised back. Ann lifted the lid to peer inside, seeing a string of pearls, an amethyst brooch, a jewelled slide.

"She left Maureen the rest of her jewellery," Josiah said, almost to himself. "Nothing for Lucy funnily enough. Her wedding ring is for Adam."

Their eyes met momentarily, then Josiah fearing that Ann would start blubbering stood abruptly, took up a

150

cigar then strode to the front of his desk. He went as though to put an arm around Ann but suddenly changed his mind, letting his arm fall to his side.

After she had thanked him and giving her promise that she would distribute the legacies that very afternoon, Ann made to leave the room.

"Do you know where I will find my son?" Josiah asked. He had his head turned from her and suddenly she had a rush of genuine feeling for him. This rare sympathy for Josiah threatening to finally make her break down before him.

"He's bought a house at Plymouth Grove," Ann said, not giving the address and departing before Josiah could detain her. That way she did not feel that she had utterly betrayed young Adam's confidences.

Although he had Ernest drive him into town, Josiah decided that he would walk the couple of miles to Plymouth Grove. The exercise would do him good both physically and mentally.

However, he was unprepared for the depression that attacked him intensely as he had, of necessity, to pass by a further scab upon the respectable face of Manchester.

The area known as Little Ireland, a district that stretched tightly across the land between Oxford Road, and Brook Street, through which the once beautiful River Medlock wound a sluggish course to the almost stagnant Irwell; its grim waters were foul, disease-ridden depths that were, he had heard somewhere, used by the Irish for drinking, as well as washing purposes.

Here it was, amongst the filth and the pigs (brought by the Irish possibly because with a pig he might evoke his agricultural past) here it was that Sarah had toiled during the cholera epidemic, against his wishes.

When he had declared his love for her he well knew a certain authority had been lost. How he had argued and remonstrated with her, amazed by her stubborn determination to stay at the Mission Hall, nursing the sick who staggered in, feeding the children, washing and cleaning and scrubbing.

"They are *my* people, I must help *my* people."

"They are *not* your people, damn you!"

But she had not listened, had gone and though young fresh-faced Irish priests caught the disease, dying in the very prime of their vocation, Sarah escaped, but she had lost the child she was carrying.

Stubborn Sarah! Like mother, like son, a perversity of spirit, their sometimes unconventional behaviour causing him impatience because he did not understand it, and he disliked what he could not understand at the bottom of his nature, which was Puritan, though he would never admit this to himself.

He did not love Adam, never could, though God knew that he had tried and even though he had failed he had always been scrupulously fair in his dealings with the boy, being at all times inclined to bend more to the boy's desires than he had ever to Maureen's, whom he loved.

However, whatever else he had or had not done he had loved his wife, loved her for the very characteristics he so disliked in their son, loved her in her still, quiet, deep moments, private and mysterious moods when she had been merely sitting quietly looking out onto the garden.

"What are you thinking about?" he often asked. A smile softly mellow.

"Nothing," the inevitable answer so that he would need to possess her for reassurance, but even in possession there was that small part of her that was not his, a secret dark corner that was closed to him. Was it Adam's? He would never know now.

Now he was in the area where his son had chosen to buy a home. It was a pleasant location with tree-lined streets surrounded by open countryside. He stood for a moment or two looking around in order to choose a house to make his enquiry as to which house was his sons. To some it would not appear a mammoth task but to Josiah, in the rigid corset of his self-imposed respectability, it was intolerable that he must go from door to door to make enquiries about his son's whereabouts. It smelt too strongly of parental failure for him to do it easily.

Before having the chance to cross the street to approach the door of a neat house, chosen by Josiah because it was set back from the street and being surrounded by bushy trees, was discreet, a coach travelling at a leisurely pace grew level with him, stopped and a low but strong voice spoke his name with authority.

"Mr Ayesthorpe," she said, "How nice to see you again!"

There was something different about the woman, a strangeness almost an air of barely concealed excitement. Although Josiah had met her but once before he was aware of the not too subtle change in her personality.

"Lady Grey," he said in polite acknowledgement and all the while uncomfortably aware of her attempting to stifle a laugh, at whose expense he could not be certain.

"Are you going to call upon your son?"

Surprised by the question Josiah nevertheless confirmed this fact to her, and being even more surprised by the fact that Lady Grey even knew the house that belonged to Adam.

"My sister-in-law told me," Lady Grey confirmed. He had thought the woman who had married William Grey had been mild-mannered. On that occasion when he had gone to Grey Manor to confront Sir William regarding his son's involvement with Maureen, she had seemed an affable pleasant woman, now he saw that his assessment had been wrong. He had been as wrong in his judgement of her character as he had been in his behaviour that night, letting them dupe him with their silken words and elegant though meaningless chit-chat, so that on his return home he had hurt Sarah. His regret was enormous, yet he knew there was nothing he could do about it, it was much too late.

Taking his leave of Lady Grey he crossed the street and took the turning into Plymouth Crescent. A tall thin darkly clad man who, it seemed, dragged his sadness behind him like a heavy sack.

She hated him; the realization coming suddenly as passion ebbed filling her with nausea.

He was arrogant, he did not fawn or plead, cajole or adore. His words were not spun from silk. He lay from her upon his back, his eyes fastened upon the ceiling reading the cornices as if they were words in a book. He was *not* grateful.

Never in her whole life had she been treated thus. Men would lie prostrate at her feet for just half the favours she had so wantonly given to Adam Ayesthorpe.

He had been gentle and tender and passionate, carrying her with him to an undreamed of paradise only to later leave her cold and lonely and feeling used.

It angered more than hurt, for she had always been the user. She wanted to make a scene but did not know how, wanted to leave but lacked the confidence to leave the bed in order to seek her discarded clothing.

Someone was hammering upon the front door, it echoed loudly through the half empty house. Adam grunted impatiently, then rolled himself from the bed to find his clothes so that he might see who dared disturb his reveree.

He said nothing to Arabella, nor did he fully close the bedroom door, she pulled the silken sheet closer around her, casting side the rougher woollen blanket and then wriggled down into the bed wretchedly.

He was too drowsy from love to be angered by Papa's appearance. He was irritated but his temper was held in check by his satiated senses. He even went so far as to let Papa into the house, only later regretting it when he saw Arabella's pink parasol, beaded bag and bonnet lying upon the floor. With feined negligence he picked them up, and set them on the table ignoring Papa's raised eyebrows and faintly fastidious shrug of his shoulder.

"I hope," he managed, "this isn't going to be a regular occurrence, I mean you calling upon me."

Papa agreed that this would not be so, then he drew the tiny gold band from the pocket of his wasitcoat, handing it to his son. The younger man held it in his palm for a long time, silently looking down at it and fighting desperately to overcome the tears that pricked his eyes. Not now, his empty soul screamed, not now while I am behaving in so deplorable a fashion that you would be ashamed of me.

At last his long fingers folded over it, and putting his hand into his side trouser pocket he pressed the ring deep into his palm, feeling its metal grow hot against his hand, enjoying the pain it was inflicting as he squeezed it tightly against his flesh.

"I intend going to Florence for the winter," Papa was saying, "then perhaps to Venice. Also I intend to visit the New World, I believe there is much to see and I have a connection with some plantation owners in Georgia and they have often asked me to visit them. It will be interesting to see cotton in its infancy."

Adam was half listening, why his father chose to tell him of his plans he did not know, certainly he could not care less what his father did or where he went. He wanted to tell his father to get out, but should he do so would mean that he must all the sooner return to Arabella, something he was most reluctant to do.

His dalliance with her had been a grave error, regret overwhelmed him. She was beautiful, he was lonely; he was a young man with all a young man's longings but more—more he had wanted to possess her because it had been something his father had wanted and had not achieved—just like his becoming an artist, but now he was ashamed of himself, utterly and absolutely.

His sensitivity would never allow him to ill treat a woman in so casual a fashion and not haunt his conscience.

"That's why I want you to take over from me," Papa finished. There was a long intense silence. Adam's mind swallowed the words, echoing them time and time again until finally they exploded in his brain, sweeping aside his indolence.

"You must be making a jest!" he snapped.

"On the contrary I am serious," Papa said, going on to explain the arrangement he had made with George Littlemoss, in just as calm a manner, confident of his ability to succeed.

He listened to Adam's refusal, to the insulting and offensive reasons, to the usual unreasonable diatribe that he had come to expect from his son; meanwhile he wandered about the room, on reaching the table he looked down at the female's belongings. They were very expensive, not the sort of clothes a woman like Rosie Meadows would buy even should she have the money. He looked at the neat purse, turning it over without knowing he did so. Near the clasp was a crest worked in gold and below the initials AF. His son had ceased to speak only his taking of deep breaths disturbing the stillness.

Josiah turned to face him; it was like looking at Sarah in a dudgeon. Wordlessly Josiah reached into his breast pocket, took out a white envelope, and placed it on the table when he saw that Adam would not take it from his outstretched hand.

"I feel you may wish to give the matter further consideration on reading that letter."

So saying Papa left, closing the front door quietly behind him. It was only after he had arrived home that the initials formed a name in his mind. Arabella Fanshaw. Weakly he sank into a chair.

"My son:

"How proud I feel just writing those words. I am a woman and I gave birth to a son, who is now a man.

"Just a few days have past since I returned from London. How exciting were the days we spent together, thank you for sharing your success with me. When I think of the long ago past it seems incredible that you, my son, have achieved so much, that I, coming from so humble a beginning could have borne such a talented child. Then it is not so surprising because any talent you have comes from your father.

"I hear your sharp intake of breath, feel the angry thud of your heart because you are grafted from my flesh and I am closer to you than to any other living person, beware my darling, for I know and do read the words carved upon your soul.

"Now I write to you without any intention of sending it by the post, when it is complete it shall be placed amongst the brief will I have this day made. I have no money to leave you, only my wedding ring, and that is

157

precious only as a sentimental token. As it was chosen by your Grandmother Ayesthorpe, you can be sure it was not expensive. Many is the time Papa implored me to allow him to buy a new ring, but that would not have been the same. I feel no guilt at being unable to leave you financially independent because like it or not one day you will inherit your father's fortune. I leave you my ring and the benefit of my experience . . .

"There are three important things in our lives. Love, honour and duty, and you cannot have the first of these without the other two.

"A man cannot feel honourable if he shirks from his duty, for he is a coward and the world does not love cowards.

"Your father and his father before him, always did their duty, no matter how painful it was to themselves, no matter that sometimes it was the very opposite of what they wanted for themselves.

"Your father is the epitome of all that is good and strong in this new society we have made for you and yours. He never, ever, once in his life shirked from his duty, and as far as I know only once behaved dishonourably, and that was with much provocation.

"For all your life he has cared for you and tried to give you certain freedoms, certainly more freedom than he ever had. I look at him now and see tiredness creeping over him, a weariness and a growing need to escape, if only for a little while.

"I will tell you something, something that you do not appear to have ever considered. I love him. I love your father. I have always loved him, immaturely and as a woman, from our very first meeting, and I will still love him at our last. I love him in all his imperfection, besides anyone perfect must be too boring to love.

"I love you too, as a child I loved you because you

were Josiah's son; when I looked at you I saw him. As you developed I loved you for your own qualities, but differently from how I loved Papa.

"My son, never in all our time together have I told you to do something. In our dealings with each other there has never been any need for that sort of discipline. I asked, you complied. I suggested, you invariably agreed because you wished to please me. However now I am telling you, if God spares me I shall be ordering you, face to face, if not you shall have to stretch your gifted imagination so that you can see me clearly in your mind's eye.

"I demand that you take over from your father. I demand that you release him from his self-imposed chains of office to do those things you have already started to do. For over twenty years he has done his duty to his father and to his family, now it is your turn.

"It is your duty to inherit his office, it is the duty of all eldest sons to do so, and you will not shirk from this duty.

"If you have any love for me at all you will obey me. It is not an easy thing I ask, that I know, you will find it difficult and painful and for a time you shall probably hate it, but by doing your duty, the duty you are honour bound to accept, you will gain character and strength.

"God or fate, whichever you choose to believe, ordained that you be an Ayesthorpe, and being an Ayesthorpe carries responsibilities. We are not Donovans or Ogdens but Ayesthorpe. From the very day Grandfather took me into his home I became an Ayesthorpe, though it took me a long time to realize it.

"If you are reading this letter then it is because I am no longer of this life but have gone—hopefully—to a peaceful rest—you will have grieved as will have Papa, but the time for grief is over now. You must begin afresh.

"Papa does not know all the contents of this letter, but

he does know that I am telling you that it is my wish that you go into the business.

"Never once has he asked me to support him in this matter, though I have known that it was his dearest wish that you join him.

"You are probably now feeling angry and resentful, that is natural. You have your art which is an important part of your life, but it is possible for you to paint even while you are doing your duty, whereas if you choose to sacrifice everything in the name of your art then you have neglected your duty, and at what a cost my son.

"You have proved to yourself that you are an artist of some merit, now prove to yourself that you can successfully shoulder the responsibilities that are truly yours. Let your father go—give him at the very least one year.

"Adieu darling and do remember that I love you,

"Always

"Mama."

His head bent, his chin rested upon his chest; the pages of Mama's letter fell from his hand onto the floor where the opening and closing of the door caused a breeze that sent them scattering to the four corners of the room.

Seven

Leek Eating Jones they called him, though he had ı
tasted a leek in years, but that was how it was; each m
had a nickname, like his mate Mick O'Grady who hᵃ
become Shady over night. Dick never now called Miᴄ
by his given name, that like so many other niceties hᵃ
been rubbed off of him.

He hated it; hated the work, the conditions, the othe
men. It was not for him, he would never become ad
dicted to the *navvy's* way of life. Living like a nomad.
following contractors from site to site, or walking on
from Lancashire to a dig in Scotland because you had
heard along the line that some of your old mates were
there and the crack was good. The crack was all important, the crack made life bearable. Good crack
—good humour and wit—was an important criteria in
this pit of living hell.

In the beginning he had had to work at any job just to
prove himself but for all his lack of height he was strong
and as wiry as a whippet, and soon he and Shady had
joined two other men making a gang of four, a financially
viable proposition always providing the others were not
lazy or too drunk all the time.

Everyone was a little drunk, even Dick; a lot of the
time there was only ale to drink, the water being fetid.
Funny, he thought, they could get beer up the line but
not fresh water. He never touched strong drink, gin or
rum and neither did the other three.

They were all in it for the money, though he suspected
the way of life had got to the other three. Just enough

brass for me and Jinny and then out of it, Dick vowed.

For weeks now he had worked knee deep in swirling mud, loading twenty tons of earth a day, the four of them aiming for a target of shifting twenty-eight wagons a day.

He had earned the respect of his peers because he had quickly learned the job. It normally took about twelve months for a man to become a fully-fledged navvy but Dick Jones had a colossal ambition and a strong determined will. He was fit and young and shrugged off the tiredness that had at first worn him down, besides the two bob a day he was able to earn in the beginning was too little to make the suffering of being in such a place worthwhile.

Now he was on about four pounds sixteen shillings a month. He lived in the communal hut and had an end bunk. Within the hut with twenty others, men, some with wives or women with whom they lived over the broomstick, their children and an assortment of dogs. There were often times after the months wages had been drunk when some of the men offered the services of their women to any man for the price of a few beers, but Dick—though he had funds aplenty—never took advantage of the situation. Apart from the strong streak of Wesleyanism within him, there was a fastidiousness, besides Shady had told him that the women were, anyway rotten with disease.

However, he did pay one of the wives, a thin careworn toothless woman of twenty-five—frequently offered up for beer—two and sixpence for cooking his dinner. Sometimes he bought a piece of beef but more often than not he walked the moors and caught his own dinner, a tasty rabbit or hare. Being country born he was an expert at poaching and sometimes on a Sunday it was a way of forgetting the hellish conditions.

Pegless Kitty cooked not only for Dick and her hus-

162

band but for three other men, Shady included. She used a large iron pot and would cook everyone's meal at the same time. This in the past had often resulted in fights because of food being mixed up, now each navvy had a coloured ribbon which was tied around a muslin bag so denoting his meal. Dick's ribbon was scarlet, given him as a keepsake by Jinny.

Yesterday one of the runners had been killed, a not rare occurrence but the first accident of that sort that Dick had ever seen.

Runners were reputed to be the toughest men on the site. They had to be strong since they ran up the cutting with a barrow strapped to their waist which was attached to a horse on the top. When the man's barrow was filled with debris a sign was given to the horse driver who would then steer the horse, hauling up the runner who had to balance his full barrow in front of him. It was dangerous hard work. Unfortunately no one was quite sure what had happened. Whether the horse faltered, or the victim of the accident had had too much drink whatever, the man lost his balance and instead of throwing his barrow to one side and jumping to the other he went over with his barrow, which as well as striking him on the head, tipped building rubble over him; when he reached the foot of the cut he was dead.

Although everyone accepted the accident with resignation Dick became depressed. Suppose he became a victim, or was maimed in one of the accidents that occurred daily, what then of his plans! And would Jinny love him were he to return to her minus a limb, or with sightless eyes. He did not wish to die, not without having ever loved Jinny, or come to that any female.

It haunted him all that week until he had no recourse but to seek out the ganger to take a leave of absence in order to travel down to Manchester to see Jinny.

The ganger was agreeable but his mates were displeased, this caused him to hesitate but only momentarily. He remembered the runner crashing down, his wheelbarrow falling upon him, his poor broken body being covered by mounds of dirt and knew that he had to return to town in order to marry Jinny. If he was going to die he was going to die as a husband. Besides he wanted Jinny to be able to take advantage of the money he had earned and as his legal spouse it would go to her.

Perhaps when he returned he would have to take any work that was offered but nonetheless he would be returning with his reputation as a hard reliable worker before him.

He walked to Ashton-under-Lyne but from there was lucky enough to be offered a lift by a carter. The man was taciturn and his only remark. "Trouble is coming," was too vague for it to register any importance in Dick's brain, which was anyway filled with thoughts of Jinny.

Within the town was such an air of hostility that even in his excitement came across to Dick. There was nothing specific, as he cautiously looked around all seemed peaceful. Groups of shabby men were congregating on street corners but there was nothing so odd about that. The town was crippled by strikes, the men thrown into a state of unaccustomed idleness would not know how to occupy their time and therefore they would cluster together to chat, and yet there had to be something else, otherwise would the hairs upon his neck bristle up, would a strong feeling of apprehension invade his mind? pushing aside the excitement the prospect of seeing Jinny had awakened.

By the time he reached Newton it was past supper time. The house appeared unoccupied so still was it, but on going around to the back he saw the glow of lights, one coming from Miss Maureen's room and the other

164

from the kitchen.

The kitchen was on ground level, a pleasant environment in which to work and built that way on Sarah's instructions. The back door let out directly onto a kitchen garden with herb borders so that now on this balmy summer evening the air was saturated with the scent of rosemary and thyme. Cautiously he peered in through the windows; Ann the old housekeeper was sitting in a rocking-chair, moving slowly backwards and forwards, her hands contentedly spread across her plump stomach, her eyes staring into space in sad concentration. Then he saw Jinny. She was sitting at the table, slowly and carefully mending some pillow slips; it was obvious that she found the task difficult and her dilemma touched him, warmly filling him with tenderness, his love overflowing.

Ann could be tart and many was the time she had told him off for hanging around waiting for Jinny. "No other house that I know encourages the servants to court. If you'd have been after one of old Mrs Ayesthorpe's maids you'd have got more than a thick ear," she had said. He had not minded these admonitions, feeling certain that Ann did not really mean them, besides, Mrs Ayesthorpe had not discouraged Jinny from meeting him.

Softly he knocked upon the door which was shortly opened by Ann. Arms akimbo she looked at him in mock contempt.

"What you doing here?" she demanded, "shirking off are you?"

"Aye," he winked, "I see you have found out my true character."

"Humf, doesn't need a lot of working out. Jinny Marsden you come here and quick about it."

She came sedately, only becoming animated when she saw who had come calling, clapping her hands like a delighted child, then blushing at being so forward in front of Ann.

"He's out," Ann said, "so off with you but be back before eleven," she said generously, giving Jane a tiny push.

They went to their secret place, beyond the cluster of rose bushes and down a slight incline to take their ease by the tiny brook that trickled through the Ayesthorpe grounds. Here he kissed her tenderly, pleased to feel her gentle response.

His pure uncorrupted Jane who radiated innocence, even more so when he compared her with the women at the camp. He would not tell her of his experiences, would not be the one to spoil her sweetness.

When he told her of his plans she expressed delight and then dismay.

"T'int possible Dickie, our Joe won't never consent. Only last week he was on at me. He has gone really funny since poor old Ellie had the babby and hasn't been able to get off the bed. He is all twisted up inside, off his head I'd say, muttering and mumbling about what he is going to do."

"Never mind, *fach*, we can marry without Joe's consent if I put you down as being of age."

"Oh no! Not to tell lies to the vicar, we can't do that Dickie, and maybe we wouldn't be married proper."

"We would, that doesn't matter. Oh Jinny, Jinny, I cannot wait any longer."

He took up her hand caressing her fingers lovingly.

"Mrs Harris has said we can have the backroom, it isn't what we want but we will be luckier than most."

"But what about me job here?"

She could not have both and was he not more important than a menial job in service. Besides he was earning enough to keep both of them and because of their natural frugal life style they would be able to marry and save for their future.

"If we don't have a family," he cautioned, imagining rather than seeing because of the dim light, her red stained cheeks.

"We can marry before I go back to the railroad and still manage to buy our own business in two years or less . . . "

"Then why rush, we can wait two years . . . "

"I can't wait," he groaned, "I might be killed."

"Be killed? Be killed?" she exclaimed, "could you be killed on the railroad?"

Jinny could not read; this he recalled with a sense of both sorrow and joy. Sorrow for he felt it a loss as crippling as having a malfunctioning limb but joy because it meant that she was unable to read any of the newspapers that might be gathering dust in the Ayesthorpe household. Newspapers that carried with grim regularity reports of the fatal accidents that were a daily occurrence on the railroad workings.

"Anyone can be killed or die at any moment in time," Dick assured, "no one knows what is around the corner. I want us to be together, to be certain that if anything happened to me all my money would come to you. I know it's silly but my mind is unsettled on this point."

It was a slight exaggeration because, although he most certainly did want his money to go to her, more importantly he wished to become a real man with her. When the prospect of death became a daunting possibility his first thoughts he admitted to himself, were regarding his lack of knowledge of women.

"Things in't the same here since Missies has gone," she mumbled. "Miss Maureen keeps to her room and Mr Ayesthorpe his study, it's gloomy, not like it was. I don't mind leaving me place but while you're away I'd like to get a job. I'd come over cracked if I din't have owt to do. Perhaps Master Adam is looking for a washer since he got his house or someone to . . . "

"You don't want to go washing for anyone," Dick interrupted, his exasperation more to do with jealousy than a dislike of her idea. Master Adam Ayesthorpe was good-looking and had on one occasion saved Jinny from a ticklish situation, thus winning her eternal devotion. He was not foolish enough to imagine that Master Adam would marry his Jinny but it was common enough for a master to wish to have a little sport with his servant and Jinny was *so* pretty!

She did not then argue against his words, leaving it be. Not that she would not approach Master Adam, only telling Dick after she had commenced the work, besides Master Adam might not have money to pay for a servant. He wasn't the richest man she knew, it was common gossip that he had only the money he earned from his painting and according to highly informed sources he was not painting.

The day they married was also the day Adam Ayesthorpe made his decision. It was a warm sunny August day that made them all believe that God was making the sun shine in order to show His approval.

Jinny had only confided in Ann her reason for leaving; time had not improved her relationship with Letitia and Ernest since both of them still suspected her of stealing from Mrs Ayesthorpe, and Mr Ayesthorpe had not taken to her either and was neither pleased or displeased by her departure.

Ann had given her a pair of well-patched linen sheets, and a new cooking pot and the cook, though she had not been told why Jinny was leaving, made her a cake, which was most appropriate had the taciturn woman only known it.

168

Mrs Harris and her daughter-in-law also part of the conspiracy would attend the old church with them. It was unusual for the working class to marry on a week day, they would not generally take time off work for such a reason, they would wait for a public holiday and be married in groups.

In the old days when Parson Brookes was the minister, rumour had it that frequently he would be marrying the wrong people to each other, no one bothered though. However, Jinny and Dick because of the secrecy of their wedding had the luxury of a private service.

There were far too many standing in idleness upon street corners, and in spite of its bustling air and its size Manchester was still a village in some respects, people knew each other, knew their families, generation from generation, and a person's business whether high or low was not guaranteed to be kept absolutely private.

Just as well-clad merchants speculated upon why young Ayesthorpe was walking in the direction of Newton, so did a poorly clad half starved man, seeing in the couple going to the old church in borrowed splendour, something that might bring a little titillation to his and his companion's wretched lives, make his way to the dwellings in order to inform the Marsdens that their little Jinny was at the church with that little Welsher.

As they came from the church in the company of the vicar and the Harrises the first person Jane saw was her brother. He was in the company of a group of men all in a similar state of poverty. Joe seemed to have some feverish disease, his eyes blazed and swollen emphasised by his skeletal head and body. There seemed no flesh upon the finger that he pointed, causing Jane to push closer to Dick, who seeing the group so obviously bent on trouble moved as if to meet them head on.

"She in't of age," Joe cried, "she can't wed without my say."

"Is that so?" the vicar asked, but softly. Jane having a clear vision of hell fire and damnation, but more even than that, of Joe hurting Dickie, confessed hurriedly, eyes looking upwards as if expecting the skies to part and God to call down angrily to her.

"Well you're too late," the vicar cried, "they are married and nought can undo it."

So saying he left them, not wishing to be part of a family squabble.

Joe Marsden looked wildly about him, almost he seemed as a wild beast, just on the verge of stamping his feet in impotence when one of his companions sought to urge him away from the scene.

"What justice," he cried, "what justice that will allow a child to marry!"

"I'm no child," Jane said at last, feeling herself becoming stronger, after all she was now a married woman, practically an equal with her brother. "I have been working since I was five," she cried, "and I'm fifteen now so you have no hold on me no more and never have had since I began to keep you and your family."

Furiously Joe leapt forward bent upon striking his sister, but Dick moving with deftness barred his way. While aware that he could easily knock Joe to the ground he could not do so, not only would it be an unfair advantage since Joe was grossly undernourished but also Dick saw that he had also been humiliated in front of his friends.

Catching his brother-in-law's collar, Dick held him lightly but with firmness, murmuring. "Leave it now, you will not lose by the arrangement, I promise you."

"You Welsh bastard," Joe snarled releasing himself

170

from Dick's grip. "I'll get you for this, one day I will and don't you forget it."

And so saying he dragged his weary body down the steps, making his way back to his hole. After looking around discomforted for a few moments his friends too shuffled off, leaving Jane to fall weakly against Dick, her tears silent confirmation of her inner despair.

It was obvious that the confrontation with her brother had taken the shine off the day for Jane. Mrs Harris had made a tea for them of cold ham and an apple tart with a pot of tawny coloured tea, and Jinny had brought out the cake the Ayesthorpes' cook had made for her, trying really to hide her depression, yet finding it difficult. Joe was, after all, her only family, and for all his faults, in spite of his selfishness and the brutality of his nature she still, in her way, loved him. Not to love him would be to commit a grave sin, the early Methodist indoctrination she had experienced at Sunday school the rule-book and guide for her way of life.

So troubled was she that she had not heard Mrs Harris telling her that she would spend the night with her daughter-in-law so that the newlyweds could have the house to themselves for one night, and it was long after Mrs Harris had gone before she missed her and turned from her task of washing the tea things at the slop stone to enquire where Dick's landlady had gone.

Dick smiled, his impudent grin that obliterated the lines of concentration from his brow, making him once more that cheeky young fellow who had followed her up Market Street, seemingly aeons ago.

"We have the house to ourselves for the night," he said. Then standing he went to her, easily spanning her tiny waist with his large capable workman's hands. Jane not understanding his words turned suddenly, her proximity spurring his emotions so that he enfolded her

171

in his arms seeking her mouth with an insistancy that she found alarming.

"Why's she left us alone?" she demanded after he had released her lips, feeling her reluctance to enjoy a deeper more intimate kiss.

"Because," he mumbled disconcerted by her manner, "because we are married," he finished.

"There was no need for her to leave us," Jinny said, turning her attention once more to the used dishes, so that Dick not having a perverse nature had no alternative but to return to his place at the well scrubbed table.

From there he watched her, she had short quick movements, that were attractive. A neat way of doing things that was a pleasure to watch. When she had done, wiping her hands thoroughly on the cotton towel, she turned to silently regard him.

"I'm not having any messing about," she said at last.

"Messing about? What do you mean messing about?"

"You know, an' if you don't all well an' good."

Clarity dawned as she went from the room, standing quickly he went to follow her out. She was ascending the stairs, later he was to regret calling her name but at that moment was too concerned to think of a better strategy.

"Jinny, we are married now, such things are normal."

"If I'd know'd you'd think like that I wouldn't never have married you. I thought you were different from our Joe."

"Jinny," he reasoned, but she had gone, leaving him alone.

The room allocated to them was at the back of the house; it overlooked the communal courtyard, privvies and refuse, an unglamorous view but not one that would disturb Jane who had been used to much worse sights,

172

although her room at the Ayesthorpes had overlooked the garden.

When she reached the room she closed the door, shattered by Dick's expectations she frantically searched for a key but there was none. Instead she took up a chair and fastened it beneath the latch. The day after tomorrow Dick would return to the railroad workings, and until then he must spend his nights where he could. She certainly would not share the bed with him now she knew what he wanted.

Pictures of her earlier life flooded into her mind. Of Joe grunting over Ellie, of the other things she had seen while working as a child in the mill, of overseers using their position to entice the older girls into storerooms or behind the clanging machinery, and then at the other extreme had been Sir William and his unwanted attentions.

In all her life she had seen no tenderness or love, the only gentleness she had experienced had been from Dick as he had courted her, but now it would appear that he was just like the rest of them.

Tears grew in her eyes, rolling down her cheeks in a steady stream. She heard him try the door, then on finding it fastened against him heard his gentle though insistent plea that she gave him entrance.

"We are married," he cried in anger and disappointment. But it was no use, she resolutely refused to open the door and he was not the kind of man who would force the door, or indeed Jane to do something she obviously did not wish to do, so in the end he turned angrily away, running down the stairs, leaving the house after slamming the front door behind him and going out into the grim streets of Ancoats, bewildered, unhappy and angry, he plunged into the first beer house that he came across.

He had thought never to enter the house again. He would have wagered all he owned against such a possibility, yet here he was in the wide hallway that faced the elegant staircase waiting while Letitia announced his arrival to his father.

Strange to be here in the house and there to be no Mama. You could not tell that Mama was not there, there were still roses in the Georgian silver vase, there was still that aroma of beeswax but there was no homely atmosphere, but he was quite willing to admit that this might well be in his imagination. His mind overflowed with pictures from the past and though he struggled to push them aside they were persistent. Mama sweeping down the stairs in a ball gown of tulle, or cream water-silk, laughing and kissing his cheeks before being swept away by Papa, or of Mama coming in from the garden, a little untidy as a ribbon had loosened throwing her curls over her shouldes, her sunbonnet swinging from her fingers.

Somewhere a door opened, he shook himself awake, shoving his memories aside and going forward to meet the man his mother had loved. The man she had given herself to and the man who had ultimately been responsible for her death.

Papa did not attempt to shake his son's hand or to greet him with more than a polite affability, nor did he invite him into his study but led him into the lounge.

The lounge was—unlike the study—full with the presence of Mama; everything in that room had been chosen by her, her colour schemes, her furniture, that quiet femininity of taste that meant even mere males would feel at home in any of her rooms.

He wondered why Papa had brought him in here instead of conducting the interview in the austere study which was just a part of Papa's personality as this room was of Mama's. If papa had done it to be cruel it was a facet of his personality that Adam had not been aware of.

They sat opposite one another and though he refused a cigar he did take a glass of port. Inside he was trembling with the effort of presenting an equable front and thought the port may soothe these tremors.

Adam did not prevaricate but came to the point immediately, stating his decision concisely, together with the terms on which he would accept his father's proposal.

If he had expected Josiah to show any emotion then he was disappointed. Papa heard him out gravely, now and again inclining his head but showing neither pleasure or dismay. Almost it was as if Papa had known all along that Adam would choose the business that he would eventually find himself, cease to play and to shoulder the responsibility of Ayesthorpe business that had been his from the moment he had been born, whether at that time Josiah had liked it or not.

Most especially he emphasized it must be George Littlemoss who supervised his training, he wanted full knowledge of all areas of the business, from factory floor to owner's office and all the other little offshoots. He would defer all final decision to his father, and would take no steps regarding expansion or for that matter in running down parts that he saw as losing money.

These would be for Josiah's decision, although Adam felt he might be compelled to make strong suggestions.

To all his terms Papa agreed. It had been his intention to spend six months showing his son the basics, then to leave him to the excellent offices of George Littlemoss now he saw that that would not work, that Adam would not let it work and so he shuffled his arrangements then casually informed his son that he would be around for three months.

Even so short a time seemed to disappoint Adam and staring at him Josiah wondered how it was that he was completely alienated from his own child. That they could not like each other could have been easily overcome but the powerful alienation that dominated his son was a force too strong to be got rid of by conventional methods. Josiah had not, in spite of trying hard loved his own father. As a child he had, but that had disintegrated when Adam had forced him to marry Sarah, and when in the end he had come to value her it had been too late to kindle the ashes of love, and yet they had got on quite well and had managed to have a reasonable relationship, although their personalities were poles apart. Adam had more in common with Josiah than ever Josiah had had with his father. They had their love of art and music, they looked quite alike and of more import they had their mutual love for Sarah. But, Josiah thought, was that not the crux of the matter.

If only he had been able to love the boy at his birth, when he was growing and forming a personality, if only he had not suspected Sarah of foisting somone else's child on him. Wearily he sighed, raking over old stony ground could not alter anything, the damage had been done, irretrievably so.

The men stood, they were of a height and made an attractive picture; a strange uncomfortable silence hung in the atmosphere, neither man knowing quite what to say in order to end the meeting, neither wishing to part on a note of acrimony.

Their discomfort was saved by the appearance of Letitia who came slyly into the room after knocking upon the door. Adam watched without amusement as her eyes devoured Papa with an adoration that was almost fanatical. The girl was so ordinary looking that he was certain Papa had never seen her as anything more than a domestic in his household, making her infatuation all the more pathetic.

Certainly by her message Adam was made aware that Letitia owed her first loyalty to Josiah, which considering that she now had become Maureen's personal maid was a sad comment on her weakness.

"Miss Maureen asked if I would take Master Adam to her room after he had finished here," she said.

Josiah raised only an eyebrow, nodded his consent then left the room at a rather hurried pace.

Adam silently followed the maid up the stairs, wanting to reprimand her for letting her mistress down but holding his tongue.

The less he became involved with the doings at the house the better it would be. The factory would be the only connection he had with his family, and that was how it was going to stay.

Adam felt it a pity that his sister took after Aunt Lucy in appearance rather than Mama. He supposed she was considered quite attractive but red hair and a creamy complexion held no appeal for him. As a child she had been much admired and had been a little spoilt by Papa. Adam had never resented her, he had not cared about her enough to have any deep feelings one way or the other.

Now as she came to him flinging her arms around him and crying upon his shoulder he felt acutely embarrassed.

"You must speak to Papa, I cannot marry George. I cannot!

Disentangling himself from her suffocating embrace he managed to steer her towards a silk-covered chaise-longue onto which she sank down, her wide taffeta skirts practically covering the whole seat so that he drew up a footstool, sitting at her feet as if he were a suitor.

"Marriage is too important a state for love to be the utmost consideration," he counselled, putting forward ideas that he had formed over years of observing other people. "Mutual background and taste are far more important so that you can be friends."

"No," she cried, "you're wrong. There has to be attraction, there must be, I could not stand George to kiss me."

Adam looked up at her, almost amused, and then realizing it was not really funny felt a sudden irritation.

"Why does Papa insist you marry George?"

Maureen did not shy from the truth, in fact it helped to be able to discuss the matter with someone else. No one had let her tell the tale of her meeting with Charles Grey and the consequences of that meeting. It was a heavenly form of torture to be able to tell her brother everything, to relive each precious moment.

When she had finished Adam sat silently for a long time; it was all so very strange, Papa forcing his adored daughter into a loveless marriage, it did not make much sense for the girl was genuinely terrified of the marriage taking place.

"He does not want me to marry Charles, this I understand, though it pains me, but why is he forcing me to marry George?"

"You are certainly very young," Adam admitted, "why is he so against Grey anyway?"

"Because his Papa once upset Mama," Maureen lisped, causing Adam to stand. Oh, why had she not held her tongue. Adam would never countenance a friendship with anyone who had upset Mama!

"But that wasn't Charles," he said at last, surprising her.

"That is what I have always said," Maureen said when

she had gained her equilibrium once more, so saying she stood, going across the room, a tall statuesque figure.

"I begged Mama to understand, I am sure she would have relented, I am certain of it—though—", Maureen hesitated, it would not be right to leave Mama's words on the subject unsaid. "She did say there was more to it."

However Maureen could tell him no more since Sarah had not been able to tell her what the other reasons were.

"If I cannot marry Charles then I wish to marry no other. Please, please Adam, I beg you to make Papa understand."

Touchingly she fell to her knees before him, clasping his hands between her own, a vision of such loveliness that in that moment he had an urge to paint her.

"All right, I will try, but Papa and I are not on the best of terms so that I doubt his being impressed by what I have to say."

"He will listen to you though. He will not even allow me to speak on the matter."

Ann informed him that Papa was in his study, therefore it meant facing the lion in his own lair. Papa's study had always been held to be out of bounds for all the family, including Mama, whose example of never going there without invitation, or indeed entering the room without prior warning, was scrupulously imitated by all the family.

Papa was reading, one of those exquisitely bound books that he collected and kept with loving care. How had, Adam wondered for the first time, grandfather and grandmother been able to produce such an offspring. His personality and desires so opposite to his parents. Grandfather had never, to Adam's knowledge, read a book, and grandmother never put her nose in anything but the lightest of romances. Who had found the seed of the art lover within him, nurtured it and shown him the

179

way, or perhaps he had found the road himself. Adam would never know, would never question Papa on personal matters thus showing an interest.

"I come as an emissary," Adam said.

"I thought you might," Papa replied, putting a book marker in his page and after closing the book placing it down upon his desk before leaning back in his chair to regard his son silently.

No one spoke for a few moments, that might have been an eternity. The silence heavy, at last it was Papa who said: "Well?"

"I thought it was for you to state your reasons."

"I do not have to state my reasons to anyone, least of all to you," he said, but quietly and without a vestige of emotion so that it was impossible for Adam to feel anything other than mild impatience at the statement.

"Isn't it a little archaic to force your daughter into marriage."

"I am archaic," Josiah said, "besides do you not believe in parents arranging marriages for their children?"

"Of course I do!" Adam answered shortly, "but not by force. She is obviously so distraught that were I her father I would leave it for the time being and later seek out another suitable prospect. At least they should like each other. We are not in the Middle Ages when such ideals were never considered."

"There is no time, and besides George is eminently suitable. He is kind and considerate, he has no vices of which I am aware."

"I agree, but Maureen is so adverse to the marriage it . . ."

"Maureen will do as she is told," Josiah rasped, "if I have to drag her up the aisle she will marry George Littlemoss."

"But why?" Adam persisted, causing Papa to slam the

palm of his hand down onto the desk's surface.

"Because she is her mother's daughter," he snapped, then paled as he felt Adam's eyes flash, "and that was not meant to be an offensive remark."

"What do you have against Charles Grey?"

"Nothing."

"Then why not look for a marriage with him."

Papa smiled without humour. Weariness invaded his body, it seeped into every cell, draining him of all his strength. He saw his son before him, young and full of energy and knew a strange, almost savage envy.

"The Greys do not wish for a match with the daughter of an Irish shanty woman."

The son exploded, his anger as he spilled cruel words from his tortured mouth, a very real and frightening thing to witness, but Josiah was too weary to care, all he saw was his own father. He of the quick temper. Josiah possessed a cold anger but Adam like his grandfather before him had a hot quick fiery temper.

"Those are not my words. I am merely quoting Sir William Grey. In all sense do you really believe the Greys would wish their only son to marry Sarah's daughter?"

"Why not?"

"Why not indeed. They should be honoured. Your mother was the rarist of women, she was the only person I ever met who was perfect.

"And man being unable to tolerate perfection must destroy it," Adam rasped.

They were steering a course directly onto dangerous ground that once stepped upon might irrevocably swallow up the tentative truce so recently struck.

"Even were the Greys to agree the match, I should not, I could not because I would be terrified that the ghost of Sarah would come to haunt me."

Adam stared at his father, hardly seeing him through the waves of hate that were threatening to engulf him.

Josiah stood, went to a decanter and poured them both a drink; placing Adam's glass into his hand he urged his passionate and rebellious child into a comfortable armchair; at the same time his mind flooded with the memory of the day of George the Fourth's coronation, the day he and Sarah had gone walking. How dreadful he had been, such a callow spineless individual and she had been so gentle, so kind, filled with warmth and love and compassion. This boy was the result of that walk, created by an act that—on his part—had only to do with selfishness. No wonder Adam was so obdurate!

"Listen to me," Papa insisted, "you loved Mama, listen then and tell me whether I am right or not. I swear that I will accept your decision."

When Adam left the study he heard a movement and looking up he saw his sister peering around the bannister. The hope so plain to read upon her face destroyed by her brother's weary shake of the head which was all, at that moment in time, he felt able to do.

On his way from Papa's house Adam experienced an erruption of feeling so acute it brought tears that he wished to call sentimental, but tears that would not be stopped. It caused him to turn off the Oldham Road and to cut across a cluster of fields and to run over the railroad tracks so to make his way to St Patrick's.

His mind was filled with Mama; how many times had she made this same journey, all alone, leaving the house silently, never complaining or asking for company. Once he had begged her to allow him to accompany her, she had had to consult Papa on the matter, and even though Papa had agreed it had rankled.

Although he had been ashamed to tell her, he had not liked it. It had been too strange, and the smell of the poor mixing with the incense had made him almost vomit.

It was enough that he never asked if he might accompany Mama again. She had never mentioned it to him, had it hurt her, his cruel and silent rejection of her childlike devotion to her God? This like so many other things about Mama he would never know, it was so unfair, there was no one to question either since he would not trust his father's interpretation of Mama's deepest feelings.

The interior of the church was an alien place to him. He did not feel comfortable amongst its altar and the statues were too garish for his pure taste. There were quite a few people kneeling, mostly old women working their beads rapidly through their fingers, mouthing words, their eyes upon the high altar with a mixture of awe and professionalism, he cynically thought.

Quietly he went to stand before the glowing candles, staring at each shrine and wondering which had been his mother's favourite and whether or not it actually mattered.

Feeling someone by his side he turned to find an aged crone watching him, a shawl of old sacking wrapped around her head and shoulders and worn with such an air of high fashion that he almost smiled.

"I wish to light a candle," he murmured, "for my mother, I'm not of the faith, I don't know what to do."

The woman tugged his sleeve, leading him to an area whose holders held more candles than any of the others.

"Our Lady," the crone muttered as if his lack of knowledge made her angry. " 'Tis the one she preferred, always she'd put a candle here, for Mary Kate, God bless her," the crone, said crossing herself.

"My mo—Mrs Ayesthorpe?" he stammered.

"Tut, Sarah—she was *always* Sarah! You haven't been to pray for her, or to pay for a Mass, none of you. Gone and forgotten by her family, but not by us, we is collecting," and so saying the old woman shuffled off, the thin piece of cardboard worked to shape her feet for shoes noiseless on the stone floor.

"Oh Mama, what a family, what a family!"

When his hands ceased to tremble he lighted three candles, one for himelf, one for Maureen and one for Papa.

Instead of backtracking over to Oldham Road he fatally made his way down St George's Road thinking to call at the dwellings to see a couple of his old neighbours, anything to pass the time until he had to be alone with his throbbing conscience. His footsteps became quicker as he heard the noise. Confused sounds of a shouting mass of people, the orderly voice of the constabulary and the sound of horse's hooves.

Then he saw it, heard the hard sound of a shot upon the still August air, his heart a terrified object inside him as if this were a living nightmare. The long ago past being acted out before his eyes. He started to run towards the mêlée as if by doing so he would find her, find and rescue the child Sarah and save grandmother from a brutal death.

It was neither a dream or an illusion conjured up by his overwrought mind, it was a riot. A stampeding angry mob had attacked the Gould Street Gas works and although the crowds were being dispersed by a company of dragoons and the local constabulary they had managed to practically wreck a police station.

There were ten thousand hungry men on the rampage, running from officialdom but on a vendetta of wrecking *en route*.

Adam found himself amidst it all, being pummelled, pushed and shoved, first by the authorities and then as he ran by the mob. Somehow he was at the centre of it, being carried away on the tide of violence that had finally erupted with volcano-like ferocity.

Terrified the powers that be, afraid of anarchy, brought out the artillery who brought a couple of six-pounder field pieces. The town would not be taken by force, its influential citizens were determined to protect property and lives.

Remarkably the two separate mobs of ten thousand and fifteen thousand strong were put down with only twenty-three treated for injuries at the infirmary, and a hundred and two arrested. Though there were two casualties indirectly.

The first was Joe Marsden, he was wounded but on his instructions was taken home rather than to the infirmary. He did not trust the doctors who he thought might be in league with the town's hierarchy and he dared not risk being sent to prison with Ellie close to death and no one to care for the babies. In this his better nature, crushed out of him by poverty and a mind crippled by bitterness came to the fore.

Within the cellar his wound festered, the poison seeping into his undernourished body, taking root and spreading so that within two days of the accident he was dead from blood poisoning, leaving a dying wife and three children to fend for themselves and being buried in the place most dreaded by all, a pauper's grave.

Adam had no alternative but to run with the mob, his feet barely touching the ground, his heart seering the wall of his chest. Being hemmed in on all sides he could not stop, if he did, the men behind would topple on top of him, neither could he move to either side since men were four abreast of him, and beyond were the chasing horses of the dragoons.

It seemed to him that he was going to collapse, to finally fall only to be trampled to death by frightened men, but as they reached Swan Street some invisible signal sent the mob separating, groups turning down into the many small streets so that Adam, following the group with which he seemed to be physically joined, ran into the area behind Smithfield Market. Once there the smaller group spread out even further. By luck rather than design Adam found himself running with a group who were not being pursued by the constabulary, though even this did not deter the others from running.

Eventually sense penetrated his tortured mind so that he forced himself to stop running and fell thankfully into a doorway, groaningly taking deep breaths, feeling the sting of hot sweat as it poured from every corner of his body, his legs like rubber.

"Did you try to run Mama? he asked out loud as he gained composure, "one of these days I'm going to kill Will Grey for you, that I promise."

Wearily he pulled himself to his feet, taking out a handkerchief he wiped his brow and adjusted his clothing, raking fingers through his sopping blond hair.

His clothing at least should hold him apart from the mob, so preventing his being arrested. For his appointment with Papa he had, thankfully, dressed with extra care, wearing his very best outfit. Like his father his mode of dress was—when he was not working —immaculate, though he possessed a flamboyance Josiah never had.

He took short cuts through innumerable warrens, each one far worse than the one previous. Now and again he met hostile glances from groups of people clustering anxiously on street corners looking for their menfolk returning from the riot. Now and again someone tossed him an angry insult, more frequently to be followed by someone saying who he was which invariably stopped the taunts but not the hostile glances.

Occasionally he met a police patrol gathered in wait for the ring leaders who were familiar to them. Once he was stopped and questioned but on giving his name was allowed to pass. It would seem that the name Ayesthorpe was a byword for neutrality enabling him to pass the mob having Sarah's protection, and the established order on the name of his father.

By a strange quirk of fate he eventually found himself by London Road and Castle Street, that elegant row of houses that had been his first home; it still retained an air of elegance but newer properties were crowding in so that the open fields once so nearby were being built upon. The town was now a sprawl without much plan or thoughtful development, a miasma of ugliness.

Here though in this graceful street a grubby knot of men were gesticulating and looking around wildly.

"Nay, nay," someone cried "they don't live here no more, an't done so for years."

As Adam stared one of the men looked in his direction, a burning look of undiluted hatred that made his blood run so cold he was tempted to run away.

"Adam Ayesthorpe," the man cried, "you is Adam Ayesthorpe, don't deny it."

"I do not deny it," Adam shouted.

"Then come here," the man cried, "for thy Granda's right poorly."

At his arrival the shabby group broke ranks. Lying down his face so grey and twisted in such agony that it took Adam all his time to recognise him, lay Grandfather Ogden. Gurgling and rasping, unable to suck air into his exhausted lungs.

"Maureen," he croaked as Adam knelt beside him, "where's my lass?"

"Grandfather," Adam murmured, reaching for the old man's hand, "Mama isn't here any more."

The old man groaned, closed his eyes as if to let his tenuous hold upon life slide; the ragged defeated revolutionaries stood around them in a hopeless group but discreetly far enough away so that they could not hear what passed between grandfather and grandson.

Wearily Sam opened his eyes once more, his eyes fully upon Adam's face.

"In me pocket," he gasped, "her things, I took em for't lads, for the movement, she would't 'ave understood no more . . ."

Someone had had the foresight to fetch a stretcher, they fastened the old man carefully down, and gently carried him to the infirmary, but it was too late.

Adam following held in his hand a badly faded pawn ticket, unsure of what it would mean but determined to retrieve whatever items were held at the pawnbrokers . .

It had rained; day and night it poured from the sky in a seemingly never-ending shower. The workings were a swirl of mud, shovelling earth in such conditions was an agony, Dick thought he would never recover from. The weight of the spade was twice as heavy because of his being up to his thighs in thick running clay. Many had laid themselves off, only the hardiest worked on. Shady, even though he worked alongside him thought Dick's brain had turned. It seemed that he worked like a man possessed by some evil force. His pace was fantastic and his hours of worked amazed the toughest navvies.

"He must have a machine inside him," someone remarked.

"He best be careful on the month end less he hurts himself by falling over his purse," someone less kind remarked.

This time around though Dick Jones was seeking not

only money but complete exhaustion. It was almost a pleasure to work so hard and to have the guarantee that when you staggered home to your hut you could fall into an exhausted stupor, oblivious to all that went on around you, and of more import able to drive from his mind the memory of his disastrous marriage and of Jinny's rejection of his rights as a husband.

Wearily in the fast fading light he made his way down from the workings to the cluster of wooden huts that was home. His moleskin trousers were wet through and mud oozed from every part of his body; disgusted by his own filth he contemptuously tore off the brightly coloured handkerchief from around his neck and tossed it down onto the ground, stamping upon it in impotent fury. It acted as a safety valve, released his anger at himself and enabled him to walk on and to remember that he was not an animal.

Inside the hut it was like a Turkish bath, overhot and steamy as those who had been working attempted to dry out their clothes. There was the usual smell of cooking, and the stench of human flesh and children and of the dogs that multiplied week in and week out.

Dejectedly he made his way towards his bunk, too tired to eat or even to think of removing his clothing. A girl was sitting on his bunk, a black shawl around her head and shoulders and a tiny lurcher puppy on her knee. Slowly she was rubbing the animal's ears, listening to its groan of pleasure.

As he reached the bunk she looked up, her eyes were very blue with no shade of grey or green to detract from the trueness of their colour. Her shawl slipped from her head causing her hair to fall in thick brown curls over her thin small shoulders. As she looked at him her naturally pink lips parted in an expression so filled with pity he was momentarily angry, which at once dissipated as the tears rolled down her pale cheeks.

Two days on the weather cleared, the Sunday was a beautiful pre-autumn day, cool and fresh, the moors empty still masses covered with purple heather for as far as the eye could see.

The landowners were out shooting game but not at the place Dick took Jinny. There all was peaceful and silent but for the sound of a lonely curlew bending its wing against a backdrop of sky as blue as Jinny's eyes.

It was good to be outside and away from the workings and jibes and the laughter, Jinny's arrival had aroused, made all the more mirthful because he had put Jinny to sharing a bed with a respectable family's two daughters, the only respectable family in the hut, or probably Dick later told Jinny, in the whole encampment.

He found a comfortable spot for them to eat their lunch between two huge gritstone boulders, they were fairly high up and below the land spilled forth towards a line of smoke that was the town of Ashton-Under-Lyne.

"In't it fresh here," Jinny remarked, taking the piece of bread and cheese he proffered and eating it like a hungry child.

"It's good, like home. One day we'll live in a nice place. I promise, *fach*."

"I don't mind where we live, Dickie, as long as we is together."

Gratefully he squeezed her hand, then quickly releasing it he stared ahead narrow-eyed.

There had not been a lot of privacy for long talks, just the essentials. The death of Joe followed by the death of Ellie, the riots, the children in the poor house. That situation though would not last long, as soon as Jinny found bigger rooms she must take them from the place, as he called it, and he would see to them.

"Oh, but not here Dickie," she had cried, "you can't

190

stay working here, it's hell on earth, I could have broke me heart when I saw you. T'int worth it."

"One more year," he assured, "then we'll have enough saved to buy a pub, is it? And it'll be a pub different from any other, wait you and see."

Although she pleaded with him he would not be swayed in his determination and nor would he let her stay. Tomorrow she must return to town, it was no place for decent folk here at the workings.

Tenderly he ran a hand over her cheek, she raised hers to press it closer against her soft skin.

"It's all right," she said softly, "I came most of all to tell you that it's all right."

Gently he smiled, using his free hand to unpin her hair, the wind caught the loose strands and played impudently amidst the glossy tendrils.

"I love you Jinny," he said.

The sound of Jinny Jones singing as she did his laundry was pleasant. He was standing feet astride looking out onto the street. Something was the matter with him; there was a lightness in his stomach, an easing of tension that had made the space between his shoulder blades less painful.

Papa had left town, taking Ernest as valet as he set out to have a look at the New World. He had no desire to see the New World, or anything other than that which he knew. Perhaps in time his opinion would change but at the moment he was well content amongst his own.

After the riots Papa had opened the factory and the ragged defeated tired men shuffled through the gates. Production was slow to start, their defeat seemed to have snapped their energy. However, Papa had said do nothing and so they passed a tense week, watching, waiting and wondering what would happen.

191

When pay day came there was a faint rumble, a surprised mumbling; the raising of spirits had not happened over night but by the end of the second week production, like moral was on the up and up.

"I gave them what they had asked your mother for," Josiah said, "you may as well start with a clear slate."

Adam was struggling with the intricacies of business and he was not quite sure that he liked it, of one thing he was certain though, it gave him a demanding interest, seemed to fire him to do more. Being fully occupied gave him little time to think and dwell upon the past. He was far too busy attempting to absorb George Littlemoss's knowledge. He was never tired in the evenings and frequently painted, painted what he wanted when he wanted and Sangster, who had not forgiven his *protégé* for deserting the art world, had thrown up his hands in horror at such a waste of talent when Adam explained that in his spare time he was painting the portraits of his family. Beginning with his unhappy sister.

Later when Jinny had returned home, taking her late brother's children with her, he put on his greatcoat and strolled leisurely into town. He would dine at his club, enjoy an after-dinner brandy, a cigar and the newspapers. Life could be enjoyable, he thought. Mama had been right, there was something good about doing your duty; an inner reward that no one else knew about, a smug little secret.

Inside the club a group of gentlemen were holding a private party, Adam paused a moment to regard them, manufacturers all who were looking forward to a future of prosperity.

"To the Lancashire witches," was the toast.

"I'll drink to that," Adam thought to himself, then made his way into the dining-room . . .